ROSCO THE RASCAL and the
HOLIDAY LIGHTS

Rosco the Rascal #5

By Shana Gorian

Illustrations by Ros Webb
Cover art by Josh Addessi

CONTENTS

CHAPTER 1

DECK THE HOMES

"Come quick, kids! I have a letter that you'll want to see!" Mr. McKendrick leaned forward in his chair for another look at the email on his screen.

It was a chilly Friday evening in early December. Ten-year-old James and seven-year-old Mandy hurried into the <u>study</u>.

Mandy knelt down on the carpet and leaned back onto her heels. James stood next to his dad's desk.

They turned to hear the jingling of metal collar tags as Rosco, their large German shepherd, shuffled into the room.

"Here, boy," said James. Rosco trotted

across the floor and stood next to him.

"What is it, Daddy?" Mandy asked. "Is it a letter from Santa?"

"It's nothing quite that exciting," said Mr. McKendrick. "But I think you're going to like what it says!"

Mandy sat forward on her knees, eager to listen.

The McKendrick family lived in the lively suburban town of Harmony. Harmony held a spectacular holiday lights contest every December.

Hundreds of people entered, but only the best entrants, chosen by a panel of experienced judges, made it onto the city's official Holiday Lights Tour.

"Listen to this, kids. It says: *Congratulations! My office is delighted to inform you that your neighborhood has been voted First Place in the Best Block category of the Official Holiday Lights Contest.*"

"First place?" James stared at the screen. "Us?"

Mandy rose to her feet. "Seriously—us?"

Mr. McKendrick spun around in his chair to face the kids.

"Yes, *us!*" said Dad, <u>brimming</u> with enthusiasm. "Why is that so hard to believe?" He pointed to the window. "First place—Best Block—our neighborhood! All of our planning, all of our hard work in the past few weeks, kids—it's finally paid off! We did it!"

Mandy threw her arms around her dad's neck and gave a hard squeeze. "Because it's the first time we ever even entered the contest, Daddy! I mean, of all the blocks—I can't believe *we* won!"

"This is very, very cool, Dad!" James patted Rosco on the back then lifted a fist to the air. "Yes!"

Rosco looked up at James, confused. What did it mean that their block was the *best*? The best what?

Mr. McKendrick swiveled around in his chair to face the computer screen again. "I thought you guys might think so. But wait.

There's more." He cleared his throat. "*As organizer of your block, we request that you inform the participants in your neighborhood to prepare for large crowds of visitors on opening night, the first Friday in December, and for all weekend evenings through the end of the month. Good luck and thanks for participating in this honored Harmony holiday tradition.*"

James walked to the window and pulled away the curtains to watch the lights on his neighbor's house blink in the dark. "Everyone at school is going to be so amazed when I tell them."

Dad nodded, glancing at James. "That's for sure."

Rosco wagged his tail. *Okay, so we won a contest, and it had something to do with the neighborhood, and with the lights he'd watched them put up recently, and it also involved lots of people.* That made sense, but he wasn't so sure about the rest of the long email. It sounded complicated.

"Wait—this means the map of our neighborhood will be posted on the Harmony website!" said Mandy. "People will come to see *our* wreaths and lights and sleighs! That means we're going to be practically famous. I have to go tell Mom!"

"Well, not quite *famous*." Dad chuckled.

Mandy dashed out of the room, hollering, "Close enough!"

James was thrilled. This was huge.

"We'll have to meet with the neighbors to make plans for opening night. It's only a week away. Plan on helping out tomorrow, James."

"Sounds good, Dad." James couldn't wait. The two of them had been working day and night on the project. First, they'd convinced all the neighbors to enter the contest, then they'd made a plan about how to decorate the block in an orderly way. Finally, they'd found a neighbor who could set up a <u>state-of-the-art</u> sound system so that music would dance in time to the lights up and down the block.

Then, James, Mandy, Mom, and Dad had

set to work on their own house. Rosco had watched as they opened boxes in the garage, stood on ladders, hooked up electrical cords, and arranged things in the front yard. Dad had climbed up on the rooftop and traipsed about as if it were nothing unusual, banging a hammer around to fasten strings of lights to the home's roof.

"We'll need Mason and his dad, too," said Mr. McKendrick. "They'll be thrilled! I'll email everyone in the contest right now."

James _cringed_. He'd forgotten for a moment that Mason Campbell, his classmate and friend who lived at the other end of the neighborhood, was also a participant in the Best Block contest.

Mason had worked as hard as any of the other neighbors, of course. He deserved to win first place as much as anyone. Then again, James thought with irritation, Mason was _always_ responsible for taking first place. He won at everything.

But as quickly as James became irritated,

the shame washed over him. He frowned. He shouldn't be feeling jealous at a time like this.

The contest was about Christmas, one of his favorite times of the year. Plus, it had been a group effort. They needed everyone on the block to help, including Mason. James brushed it all aside. There were better things to think about—good things.

For instance, it was one of James' and his sister's favorite December traditions to load up in the minivan at night, turn on the Christmas music, and drive around to see the winners of the Holiday Lights Tour. Every year, the kids would sip hot chocolate and sing along to carols while Dad drove. Mom would exclaim over the displays and laugh the loudest at Mandy's corny Christmas jokes.

This year, people would drive around to see *his* neighborhood and his house!

First place? He still could barely believe it. People came from miles around to see the Best Blocks. Many would get out of their cars and stroll the sidewalks. Enjoying the Holiday Lights Tour each year during the month of December had become a beloved tradition in Harmony. An entire neighborhood decked out in holiday lights, after all, was the closest thing Harmony had to a winter wonderland.

Yet, although the winters were always chilly, they weren't usually *freezing* cold. It wasn't usually cold enough to snow, and when it did, only a few inches fell.

That might have been why the people of Harmony went all out with holiday decorations. Colored lights, <u>inflatable</u> snowmen, and battery-powered dancing polar bears could make it feel like Christmastime almost as well as snow could.

Mandy <u>bounded</u> into the <u>study</u>. "Mom says I can start making the sign for the hot chocolate stand tonight!"

"That's great, honey," said Dad. "No time like the present."

"The present—I get it! Like a Christmas present!" Mandy jumped up and down.

"Something like that," said Dad.

James groaned.

"I can't wait for Christmas *presents*!"

9

Mandy said.

Mandy and James had decided that they were going to open a hot chocolate stand if their block made it onto the tour. Mandy had always wanted to run a lemonade stand, but hot chocolate would do just fine.

"Mom says the poster board and markers are in the kitchen. James, can I make the sign by myself?"

"Sure, go ahead," said James. "I'll be busy helping Dad."

"Thanks!" Mandy could barely stand still. "You know, this might just be the best week of my life, *ever*. First, I have the train parade at school, and then, the Holiday Lights Tour right here on our very own street!"

Dad spun back around in his chair. "Oh, that's right, Mandy! Is your train car ready for the school parade?"

"I'm still working on it, but I have until Wednesday."

"Well, you certainly have enough holiday spirit for all of us."

Mandy giggled.

"Except maybe for Rosco." Mr. McKendrick winked and grabbed a pair of costume antlers from a basket on the desk. "Here, James. Try these on him. He's looking glum. Maybe he could use some holiday spirit."

Indeed, Rosco wasn't feeling quite as merry and bright as they were. He was still confused. *Can someone explain this contest in words I can understand, please?* Rosco sighed and sat down on the floor.

But it wasn't to be. Instead, James placed the fuzzy antlers on Rosco's head and tucked the headband behind his soft black-and-brown ears.

Mandy squealed with delight. "He looks so cute—like a real reindeer, almost!"

Rosco pawed at the headband and shook his head from side to side. *No thanks, guys. This isn't helping me with Christmas spirit—not even a bit.*

With a hard shake, the antlers fell to the

floor. *Keep that off of me, please.* He shook himself and hustled across the room where he lay down to rest. Rosco wasn't a big fan of costumes.

"Aw, I'm sorry, boy," said James. "We won't try it again." He walked over and petted Rosco's back.

Rosco took a deep breath and put his head down on his paws. *Good. Thanks. And don't worry about me. I'll find some holiday spirit on my own.*

Although the antlers hadn't helped Rosco, in fact, there was no shortage of holiday spirit in Harmony. Hundreds of houses entered the contest, and first-place ribbons were awarded to the Most Outrageous, the Most Traditional, and, of course, to the Best Block.

Last year James' favorite house had been the winner of the Most Outrageous category, and it wasn't just because of the lights. A life-sized reindeer and Santa Claus sat on the roof. Elf statues stood on the porch. Kid-sized trains, giant snowflakes, and dancing penguins filled the yard.

The lights on the house danced in rhythm to the Christmas music playing in the background. The whole effect was stunning, and now James would be responsible for something like that!

The Best Block award was only given out when a neighborhood worked together to decorate an entire block. At least twelve houses in one area were required to participate in order to enter the contest. Incredibly, *sixty* houses in James' neighborhood were participating! It was more than just a block—it was *six* blocks!

James could barely wait to tell his friends at school on Monday. He couldn't wait to see their faces.

CHAPTER 2

BLOCK PATROL

Late the next morning, excitement filled the chilly air as James, Mandy, and their dad met with the neighbors.

"Thanks for meeting out here, everyone. Now, let's get down to business," said Mr. McKendrick. "First of all, my wife and I decided to host a little celebration. The contest judges visit each winning block to make sure things are running smoothly every year on opening night, and I thought we might share our Christmas spirit with them while they're here. So I invited them over."

"Good idea, Dan," said Mr. Campbell, Mason's dad.

Mr. McKendrick looked around the group. "My wife makes delicious cookies and eggnog this time of year. You're all welcome to stop in on opening night, too."

After the neighbors thanked him, they divided up the list of tasks for each night of the tour. Then Mr. McKendrick waved his hands. "Listen up, everyone. I have a few more things that the officials wanted me to share with you."

The group gathered in. "Opening night will be the most important night for our block, because that's when the judges will be watching very closely. If things aren't shipshape around here, the city won't hesitate to let us know. Apparently, it's a very big deal."

"That happened about three years ago," said Mr. Da Costa, who lived next door to the McKendrick family. "It was over on the west side of town. I was there that night!"

Mr. McKendrick turned to address Mr. Da Costa. "What happened that night, Jim?"

"It turned out they hadn't prepared well for the crowds. There were no signs to point drivers which direction to drive through the tour, and too many cars were parked on the streets inside the neighborhood. Traffic practically came to a standstill!"

James and Mandy were surprised. Mr. McKendrick listened closely.

"And then lots of folks didn't leave their lights on, so almost half of the Best Block was dark!"

Several neighbors gasped.

"The city received so many complaints that they made new rules for the following year. Nowadays, if a neighborhood doesn't run its opening night well, the officials can remove them from the tour—completely."

The group exchanged a worried look.

Mr. McKendrick nodded. "I remember it was a huge embarrassment for that neighborhood. And that explains why the rules are so strict."

Mr. Campbell spoke up. "So if they think

we're not operating at a first-place level, they can take away our first-place status, just like that?"

"Just like that," said Mr. McKendrick, snapping his fingers. "The winner of the Best Block represents all of Harmony, so the city wants to be sure that we live up to its standards. You know—keep the public happy and put on a really good show."

"Well, I'm sure we can live up to Harmony's standards if we put our best foot forward," said Mrs. Benton, the retired woman who lived on the other side of the McKendrick's house.

"Agreed, Elizabeth," said Mr. Campbell. Everyone nodded. Mandy gave Mrs. Benton a wide smile, nodding.

"Great, then. It's going to be a lot of work, but a lot of fun!" Mr. McKendrick finally <u>addressed</u> the kids in the crowd. Most were younger than Mandy. "Kids, we need your help too, keeping the yards nice and neat, helping your parents with whatever they ask.

So do your best to make the neighborhood proud." The children turned to each other and chatted excitedly.

Then Mr. McKendrick turned to James and Mason. "Boys, I've got a job that I'd like you to do together on opening night, since you're older than the others. It's going to be extremely important. What do you say?"

James raised an eyebrow. He wasn't crazy about working closely with Mason. Plus, opening night was starting to sound like a lot of pressure. But there were too many people around for James to refuse. He'd just look rude. "Uh, sure Dad. Okay."

"Great. How about you, Mason?"

"Sure, Mr. McKendrick. I'm in!" said Mason. "What's the job?"

"Block patrol!" said Mr. McKendrick.

"What does that mean, Dad?" James asked.

"It means you'll be the eyes and ears of this operation—the soldiers on the front line!"

James and Mason exchanged a questioning look as Mr. McKendrick continued. "Since it's hard to get back and forth around here in a car on a busy night like opening night, we'll need people to go on foot or on a bike. You two can do that! You can patrol together and if you find a problem that you can't fix by yourselves, you can report it to me." He took two handheld radios from his jacket pocket and handed one to each of them. "I'll have one of these, too."

James pushed a few buttons on the walkie-talkie as he listened to his father. He liked the sound of this job—a lot—but he wasn't so sure about working with Mason.

"Then I'll alert the homeowners by phone so they can fix any problems," Mr. McKendrick continued. "I think we can keep things really tight that way."

Mason nodded eagerly. "Sounds great, Mr. McKendrick. What kind of problems are you talking about?"

"You know, if someone's lights go out—

things like that. We can't keep an eye on our displays at every moment of the night, after all. I'll be entertaining the judges at our house, so I can't patrol that night."

Mr. Campbell spoke up. "I think it's a great idea to give the kids a little responsibility, Dan. And of course, we'll be close by if you need us, boys."

"Thanks, Dad," said Mason. "You can count on me."

"You'll do a great job, Mason. You too, James," said Mr. McKendrick.

"Uh, thanks, Dad." James was torn. Patrolling the block sounded really cool, but things usually felt like a competition with Mason. James wasn't used to being on the same *team* with him even though they hung out with the same group of kids at school. Besides, Mason always took over, acted like the boss of everything. James really didn't want him doing that this time. He chewed on a fingernail, thinking.

Mr. McKendrick clapped his hands and

rubbed them back and forth. "All right, now. Why don't we all get back to work before this whole Saturday gets away from us?"

Mr. Benton spoke up. "Hold on Dan. How about if they patrol a few times after school next week, too? It'll be good practice."

"That's a great idea, Charles," said Mr. McKendrick. "Got that, boys?"

CHAPTER 3

BETTER NOT POUT

Monday morning arrived. Mason stood outside the classroom talking to fellow fifth graders Leo, Asher, and Ian. "Guess what? You guys won't believe this."

"What?" asked Ian.

"My neighborhood was awarded Best Block in the Holiday Lights contest! The very best block—first place. So that means my house will be on the city tour this year!"

"For real?" said Ian.

"Dude," said Leo, "that's so cool!"

"Yeah, I know! The lights look so awesome! Everyone on my street and a bunch of other streets are in on it. It's going to be *epic*!" Mason raised both arms in the air. "You guys *have* to come see it!"

"Wouldn't miss it," said Asher. "Congrats."

"I'm in," said Ian.

Mason went on. "It's going to be almost like—like a whole *show*, with music playing in time to the lights, and *everything*!"

Leo switched his backpack to the other shoulder. "I went to see the Best Block last year. It was really cool. I wish I lived on your block! You're so lucky!"

"Wait—actually, I have an idea!" said Mason. "Why don't you guys all come and help? James and I were assigned block patrol on Friday night and I'm sure we could use the help. It'll be fun!"

As the boys settled the plans, James arrived. "Hey guys, what's up?"

Mason explained what had been decided, and James' jaw dropped—Mason had already told them the news *and* invited them?

"So we'll all meet at my house first on

Friday night." Mason high-fived Ian. "Is that cool?"

Leo and the others nodded, smiling and waiting for James to respond. But James was <u>tongue-tied</u>. "Uh..."

Mason had already taken over the whole thing *and* made himself the boss.

James hadn't really wanted to share the job with anyone, and now he had to share it with everyone. But once again, he'd only sound rude if he said so. Instead, he stood there, swallowing hard, his cheeks beginning to burn. "Uh, okay. Cool."

Over the hum of the hallway chatter, the bell rang. The students filed into the classroom and took their seats.

"This is gonna be really fun, James," said Leo. "Can I use the walkie-talkie, too?"

James sighed, nodding, and walked into the room with the last of his classmates. He plopped his books down on his desk and sat at his seat, which was next to Mason's.

"Psst! Mason, you couldn't wait until I

got here? I thought we were going to tell everyone together."

James had thought all weekend about how he'd tell his friends the big news. "I mean, my gosh—my dad's in charge of our whole block! Without him, the tour wouldn't even be happening in our neighborhood!"

"You weren't here yet, James. The bell was going to ring. I couldn't wait any longer."

"I wasn't even late! You could've waited ten more seconds!" said James. "And—you invited them all to patrol, too? Why'd you go and do that?"

"The more the merrier. The block is huge, James. It'll be fun."

"But my dad picked us two, not a bunch of our friends. They don't even live on our block," said James. "It's a job, not a party. We can't have a bunch of guys goofing around."

"No one's going to be goofing around," said Mason. "Trust me. It'll be fine. And by the way, it *is* kind of a party. It's a holiday lights tour! It's supposed to be fun."

Miss Fitzgerald tapped on her desk. "Good morning, students," she said. "It's time to open your science books."

James glared at Mason.

Mason shot back with a questioning look, motioning with his hands. *What do you want from me?*

James shook his head and sighed. It seemed like Mason always did this kind of thing—made everything about *himself.* James should've expected it. He opened his textbook and tried to concentrate on what Miss Fitzgerald was saying but his thoughts kept interrupting.

Mason was the kid whose baseball team had beaten him to the championship last spring. Mason was the kid he always competed with for the best scores in math. Mason was the kid who had won first place in the talent show playing a shiny, black electric guitar. James wished he could play the guitar.

The weird thing was that he liked Mason well enough. Everyone did. Mason wasn't a bad kid. He was nice enough—popular, outgoing, respectful—most of the time.

People always seemed to want Mason to win, to go first, to be team captain, to get the lead role, to be at every birthday party. They expected it from him. Even the teachers liked him best.

And because Mason was so smart and so talented, he just assumed he was always in charge of things. James was definitely not looking forward to working with him now.

Today, Mason had already found a way to steal the show, and it was only nine a.m. James chewed on his pencil, trying to focus on Miss Fitzgerald's voice before he missed the whole lesson.

CHAPTER 4

GUILTY AS CHARGED

Later that afternoon, Mandy opened the front door and clapped several times. "Rosco!" she called. "Come back!"

Goosebumps ran down her arms as the chilly late-afternoon air met her face. When she didn't hear the jingle of her dog's collar, she clapped again. "Rosco! Come on home, boy!"

"Mandy, will you shut that door, please?" Mom called from the kitchen. "If you hold it open any longer, you might as well invite Jack Frost in for dinner."

Mandy closed the door, grinning at Mom's joke. She shifted to the living room window, where she peered out through the curtains. *Gosh, where is he?*

* * *

A few blocks away, Rosco tip-tapped down the sidewalk, taking a walk. He had wanted answers to his growing list of questions and thought he might find some if he went exploring.

A little over an hour ago, after a long rest, he'd woken to find Mandy sitting on the floor of the living room, adding some finishing touches to a piece of poster board. He thought it might be the perfect chance to sneak outside and take a look around. She'd been so involved in her work that she hadn't even looked up when he left the room.

He'd slipped out the back through his doggie door. But he still hadn't found any answers—only more questions. Like, why were all the yards filled with fake deer and elves and kid-sized trains? They weren't there a few weeks ago.

After a short time, Rosco had come upon a house with an unusually <u>festive</u> fence. The suburbs of Harmony were known for their wide, grassy lawns, tall trees, and cozy homes with big backyards. They were even known for the little brick walls that lined the sidewalks in some neighborhoods. But one thing they weren't known for was their fences. In fact, most yards in Harmony didn't have fences separating one home's backyard from another. So Rosco was especially curious when he saw this one.

Oddly enough, the fence appeared to be made of <u>decorative</u>, giant, plastic, red-and-white peppermint sticks, and it enclosed the whole front yard. He stopped to investigate. This fence wasn't here last week. Why was it here now? It didn't make sense.

A lot of things didn't make sense, for that matter. Like, what was going on with all the outdoor lights? Weren't people satisfied with the darkness anymore? And what exactly was this contest everyone was talking about? Rosco didn't understand.

The peppermint gate was open, and just inside the fence, a bit of movement caught Rosco's eye. A tiny sparrow flitted about from grass to bush to bench, looking for a worm.

Although birds were hard to catch, Rosco

loved to chase them. He quickly forgot about the candy fence and dashed through the gate, sprinting toward the bird.

But luck was not on Rosco's side. Running at full speed, a snowman statue appeared directly in his path. He tried skidding to a stop, but it was too late. Rosco smashed into the snowman, and it <u>toppled</u> to the ground, breaking into three giant plastic snowballs. As the snowballs rolled across the grass, Rosco looked up just in time to see the sparrow darting off.

Missed—again! He stood up and scanned the yard, then shook off his disappointment.

"Rosco!" Mandy's voice echoed faintly from a distance. "Where are you?"

Ah, well, Rosco thought. *I knew Mandy would be looking for me soon enough.* Exploring the neighborhood would have to wait. Rosco wasn't one to keep his owners waiting—if he could help it. Certainly, on this quiet Monday afternoon just before dinnertime, he could help it.

He brushed himself off once more, and took one last look at the mess he'd made. It was definitely time to go. At the gate, he stuck out his tongue and gave the peppermint fence a quick lick.

It didn't taste like candy. It didn't taste like much of anything, as it turned out. So he trotted through the gate and started down the cold sidewalk toward home. *Now why would anyone build a fence that looks like candy, especially if it doesn't taste good?*

Dusk was just beginning to settle in, but a colorful glimmer brightened the late afternoon as neighbors switched on their Christmas lights. *Very pleasant.*

From behind him came another familiar voice and the sound of bicycles pedaling down the street. "Hey look, there's your dog, James!" Mason called.

"That's strange," said James. "He's not usually out here alone."

Rosco turned and stopped to wait. He hadn't realized that James was out riding.

James and Mason rolled their bikes to a stop. "Hey boy, whatcha doin' out here?" said James, puzzled. "It's almost dark." He turned and looked at Mason. "Rosco should be at home right now. I wonder what's up?"

Just out for a little walk, Rosco thought, <u>imparting</u> his most trustworthy smile to the boys. He let his tongue drop down as he panted. *No need to worry about me.*

"Hmm," James said, glancing about but finding nothing unusual. "I guess he's fine."

"He's not up to any trouble this time?" Mason teased. "You sure about that?"

"He's not *always* up to trouble, Mason," said James, straightening his shoulders. "Maybe he's just getting some fresh air. Who knows?"

"Then what's that silver glitter all over his back?"

James tilted his head to inspect Rosco's fur.

Mason gave James a sly grin. "Is he just being <u>festive</u>, or do you think maybe he got into someone's Christmas ornaments?"

<u>Guilty as charged</u>, Rosco thought. *Sorry, guys. I should've been more careful.* He'd had a run-in a few streets back with some sparkly lawn statues—lovely ladies made of fake stone and covered in silvery glitter with their mouths wide open as if they were singing. They looked so real, except for the

glitter, that Rosco thought it seemed odd that no sound was actually coming from their mouths.

The incident involved a pesky little squirrel that Rosco chased across the lawn. Doing so caused him to knock over the ladies, which sent glitter flying in every direction.

He was sorry to admit that after a long, hard chase, the doggone little squirrel had managed to outwit him, just as the sparrow had done. *Oh well, better luck next time.*

"I don't know if he got into anyone's Christmas ornaments," James said. "But Mandy was finishing the sign for our hot chocolate stand at home. Maybe she spilled something on him."

"Sure, James. Whatever you say." Mason winked.

"Just because he's out here with a little glitter on his back doesn't mean he did something wrong," said James.

"At least nothing we know of," Mason teased.

"You don't have to pick on him all the time, Mason."

"I'm not picking on him. I'm just kidding around. It's true, anyway. He's always getting into something. I bet he knocked over that snowman, too. The gate was open. There's no one else around."

"Humph." James backed up and turned his front tire to face the other direction.

"Anyway, if we're out here patrolling, then we should be looking for trouble, right? If your dog's causing trouble, then he needs to be stopped."

Rosco lowered his head and stared at the ground. Did Mason really think he was *that* bad? Those were just accidents. He didn't mean to knock anything over.

From a distance, Mandy's voice interrupted, a bit louder this time. "Rosco, where *are* you?"

"That's my sister," said James, sighing. "I'd better get Rosco home before she sends out a search party." He rolled his eyes and placed a foot on the pedal. "Come on, boy. Let's go."

Rosco thought he ought to do as he was told before they noticed anything else he might have done wrong. *I shouldn't have chased that bird or that squirrel.* He marched over to James and waited for his next command. *I'd better be more careful next time. Sorry, James.*

"My mom's probably looking for me by now, too," said Mason. "But I'll try to put that snowman back together before I go home." He glanced in the direction of the candy stick fence. "Man, that fence looks so good I wish I could eat it!"

"Yeah, me too," said James.

Rosco fixed his eyes on the sidewalk ahead, trying not to feel as awful as Mason made him sound. *They sure are concerned with the way things look around here, aren't they?*

"Anyway, I think we're in pretty good shape for Friday," said Mason. "Don't you?"

"Yeah," said James. "I saw a few other small things, but we can get to them tomorrow."

"Okay, see you in the morning." Mason turned his handlebars and headed toward home.

"See you," James replied. "Come on, boy." James began pedaling. Rosco followed, quickening his pace to keep up with the bike.

A few minutes later, James and Rosco reached the house. Even from the driveway, Rosco could smell Mom's cooking. *Mmm. It must be dinnertime. Now, that makes me feel better. Chicken, I think?*

Rosco glanced next door and was delighted to see that his best pal, Sparks, a Pug, was perched in his usual spot in the living room window. Charles and Elizabeth Benton, the retired couple next door, were Sparks' owners. The little dog yipped pleasantly through the window when he saw his friend. Rosco barked back.

Careful to avoid the electrical cords that

were plugged into the outdoor socket, Rosco trotted up the stairs. The charming lights and decorations on their house gave it a warm and welcoming feel.

"There you are, boy," Mandy said, placing her hands on her hips. "Where have you been? I've been looking all over for you!"

Shuffling in, Rosco took a whiff of the glorious smells coming from the oven. "What's that all over your back, Rosco?" said Mandy. "You're sparkling."

Rosco ignored the comment and continued toward the kitchen.

"It's time for dinner, kids," Mom called. "James, did you take Rosco with you on your bike ride? We didn't know where he'd gone."

"No, I didn't. Mason and I were just checking to see if we could find anything that needs to be done before Opening Night, and there he was."

Hmm. Wish I knew what opening night means. Rosco wagged his tail. *Maybe it has something to do with the email Dad read to the kids?*

Mandy took Rosco's bowl into the pantry. *Ah well, it doesn't matter right now.* Dinner smelled great. He had worked up an appetite. *I'll go looking again tomorrow.*

Mandy returned from the pantry with Rosco's bowl. *Mmm, dinner,* Rosco thought, welcoming the <u>distraction</u>. He licked his chops and sniffed at the air.

Mandy bent down and slid the dog bowl in front of him. "There you go, boy."

But it wasn't Mom's cooking. *You're kidding me—this again?* His eyes drooped at the sight of the brown nuggets of kibble in his bowl. *<u>Aw, fiddlesticks</u>.*

CHAPTER 5

ALL BY HERSELF

On Tuesday afternoon, Mandy knelt on the living room floor decorating her train car for the Holiday Train Parade. Candy wrappers and empty plastic bags covered the tile. She pressed her last gumdrop firmly into a dab of glue on the side of a large, brown, cardboard box. She'd had a busy week with art projects.

Perfect, she thought, sizing up her work. A moment later, a gumdrop slid slowly down the side of the box. Mandy's smile faded.

Uh-oh. She reached for the glue and applied another dab. It wasn't holding very well, but the hot glue gun would help.

"Mom, where are the giant lollipops?"

Mandy called. "I'm ready for the wheels!"

"They're on the dining room table, honey!" Mom replied. "I'll be there in a minute!"

Setbacks were not going to get Mandy down today. She sifted through a mountain of Mom's holiday projects on the table. "Found them!" she called, and went back to work.

Mandy plugged in the glue gun just as Mom entered the living room.

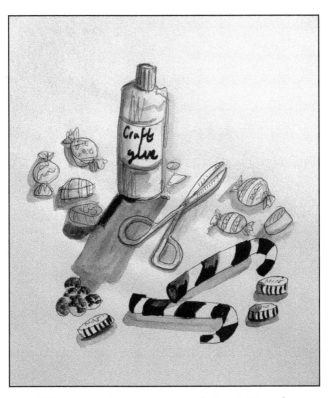

"Honey, what are you doing? You know you're not allowed to use that by yourself," said Mom.

But Mandy had already made up her mind. "I don't want any help. Remember? I told you."

"Yes, I remember, but I told you that you're not old enough to use that yet," Mom said. "It gets really, really hot. I don't want you to burn yourself. I'll just dab the glue on and you can—"

"But Mom, this will be my *third* time making a train car for the parade," said Mandy. "I can do it. Plus, second grade is my last chance. I want to do it by myself this year!"

"I understand that, honey, but I'm sorry, you may not use the glue gun by yourself. Kids burn their fingers far too often."

Mandy breathed in slowly then breathed out through her nose.

"Fine," she said, crossing her arms and pointing her nose in the air. "I'll just use regular old glue from the bottle if that's the only thing you'll let me use *by myself*."

Mom raised an eyebrow and stared at Mandy for a long moment. Then she unplugged the glue gun to let it cool, turned on her heels, and walked out of the room, shaking her head back and forth.

And that was that. Mandy would have to make some adjustments to her plan, like using a *lot* of plain old white glue instead of just a few dabs of hot glue. Maybe her train car wouldn't look as perfect as some of her friends' cars, but at least she would have made it *all by herself.*

Mandy had waited for months for this. Last week, she told her mom she was making a gingerbread car instead of a gingerbread house. Mom loved the idea and had taken her out to buy candy and ribbon for the straps.

The large cardboard box they found was already the right shade of brown, but the project still required a lot of work.

Mandy had carefully arranged gumdrops, peppermints, and candy canes to represent the windows and doors. She'd lined the edges with white paint to look like icing. Now, all she needed to do was glue on the four giant lollipops so they'd look like wheels on a steam engine.

Rosco was dozing nearby. Every now and then, he'd wake up, shift his eyes around without lifting his head, and then drift back off to sleep. He wanted to be sure he wasn't missing anything.

"This should still work, Rosco," Mandy said, holding the bottle of glue upside down and giving it a squeeze. She liked having her dog around while she worked. He never interrupted her or told her what to do.

What in the world is she doing? Rosco <u>gaped</u> at the box for a second, but the drowsiness got the better of him and he drifted back off to sleep.

Mandy could hardly wait to show her friends what she'd made, and she would get the chance to very soon because parade day was tomorrow!

In the morning, the kindergarten, first-grade, and second-grade classes would line up and march across the school campus in their decorated train cars.

It was a yearly tradition. Mr. Han, the principal, would lead the way in his blue-and-white striped conductor's hat. Parents would snap photos and wave while teachers and students cheered. Afterwards, hot chocolate and cookies would be passed around before the children returned to class. Mandy loved Holiday Parade day.

Several minutes later, Mandy carefully let go of the lollipops, which were now sticking to the side of the box. "There," she said. "The wheels are finished. See how easy that was, Rosco?"

Hearing his name again, the sleepy dog lifted his head and glanced over at her. He twitched his ears and laid his head back on the floor, closing his eyes.

Mandy went to the dining room table and found the ribbons she had cut earlier. She brought them back to the living room and held them over the box.

"Wow," Mrs. McKendrick said, strolling back into the room. "It looks like a real gingerbread house—I mean, car. Great job."

"Thanks." Mandy was enjoying herself again.

"I found the stapler," said Mom, kneeling

down. Where do you want the straps to go? How about right there?"

"That's okay. I can do it myself," Mandy said politely. She had decided not to be mad at Mom. Mom was only doing her job. And besides, Mandy was in a good mood and she wasn't going to let a little glue gun trouble get her down today. "I'm still allowed to use the stapler, right?"

"Yes, of course you are," said Mom, handing her the stapler.

"Thank you," said Mandy.

Mandy set one ribbon on the floor and held up the other in front of the box. "I'm going to put it right here." She squeezed the stapler over the cardboard until it made the clicking noise. "Perfect." She reached for the second ribbon.

"Wait, honey!" said Mom. "Don't you want to measure so they'll be the same length across your shoulders?"

"Nope! I know what I'm doing. They don't need to be that perfect, anyway."

Mom raised an eyebrow.

Mandy laid the second ribbon against the box and stapled it to the other side without pausing to line up the ribbons. "It'll be fine. You'll see, Mom."

"I'm sure it will, honey. I just thought maybe—"

"Don't worry about it," said Mandy, standing back to admire her work. "It's perfect—just like this."

Mom blinked several times and sighed. She forced a half-smile, then turned and walked out of the room, still talking. "Fine, young lady. Have it your way. I admire your can-do attitude, even if your measuring skills leave something to be desired."

This looks great, Mandy thought. Tomorrow could hardly come soon enough.

"Look, Rosco. Don't you just love it?"

Rosco raised his head again and stared at the project, still trying to figure out what the box was for. He let out a wide yawn.

"I'll take that as a yes," Mandy said.

"Thanks, Rosco. I love it, too."

All right, he thought. *I'm awake now.* He rose to his feet and stretched, then treaded over to inspect the box. Why, it was food; candy, as a matter of fact. Delicious, sweet, colorful candy stuck all over the box in patterns. He sniffed at it with interest.

"Rosco, don't even think about it," Mandy warned. "This is for school! You can *not* eat it." She placed a steady hand on his back.

Apparently, Mandy did not wish for Rosco to take a lick of a lollipop.

Okay, fine. Rosco stepped back. Why would anyone glue food to a box? Why would Mandy bring a box covered in candy to school? What was she planning to do with it? Goodness, why was everyone acting so strange around here?

CHAPTER 6

TANGLED

Wednesday morning arrived. Rosco looked out the living room window. He was ready to investigate again today and silently promised himself that there would be no more <u>incidents</u>. He would explore as much as he could, but would be careful to stay on the sidewalks and avoid all trouble.

But he wanted to get on with it. He paced about inside the house. Dad had left for work half an hour ago. Mandy and Mom were in the driveway putting Mandy's candy-covered box in the back of the minivan. Rosco still wasn't sure why. She'd even tried it on this morning as if it were a costume, like the ones the kids wore for Halloween. *Maybe there's going to be a costume party at school today?*

James had chosen to take the school bus and was waiting at the bus stop with a dozen or more children at the far end of the street. Rosco peered out the window at them. They were laughing and talking. It looked like fun.

Rosco slipped out through the doggie door and into the backyard. He'd watch the kids from the front porch until the bus arrived.

Rosco rounded the house and stopped in his tracks. There sat a squirrel, just like the one he saw on Monday near the statue ladies. It darted directly in front of him and sped across the lawn into the next-door-neighbor's yard.

Rosco held his breath. When the squirrel finally stopped on the grass, it sniffed at the air.

Rosco stood perfectly still and watched. He hadn't expected to see such a fast-moving little critter so soon this morning. It almost seemed as though the squirrel was daring him to chase it. Rosco's nose twitched and his legs itched—he wanted to run! *Why, now, it's just sitting there, right in the middle of the lawn!*

But he remembered how James had defended him when he'd knocked over the lawn decorations. Rosco knew that he'd better stay put and stay out of trouble, especially since James and the other kids were nearby at the bus stop. What if he knocked something else over? *You mustn't chase it. You promised,* Rosco thought, trying to hold himself back.

However, the force of his instinct was just too strong. That doggone little critter was just teasing him, sitting so still. He had to make chase—he just *had* to.

Forgetting his promise, he dashed across the frosty grass as if this fuzzy little squirrel were the only thing that mattered in the entire world. *Look out, squirrel—I'm coming to get you!*

But it wasn't going to be easy. An elaborate checkerboard pattern of wires was strung across the neighbor's yard—green wires about six inches off the grass. The lights made for an amazing ground-level display at night.

But since they were green, they were almost hidden because the lights were turned off in the daytime. Rosco had forgotten about them completely—they were so well disguised against the snowless grass.

Rosco raced at full speed toward the squirrel. *Oh, the joy of the chase!*

But Rosco didn't see the wires until he was almost on top of them. His foot caught on a wire, and he was going so fast that he couldn't stop. He tripped on one wire, and then another, and another!

Like a boulder launched from a slingshot, Rosco slammed into the <u>mishmash</u> of tightly <u>staked</u> lines and sailed backwards, landing flat on top of them.

Down the street, waiting at the bus stop,

Mason saw the whole thing. His jaw dropped open. "Oh my, gosh, James, your dog just went flying across Mr. Da Costa's yard! Did you see that?"

"I saw it, all right," said James, eyes wide.

"Look, you guys!" Mason chuckled. "Did you see James' dog? He went after a squirrel and got caught in the wires! Look at him!"

A few of the kids had noticed and were already giggling. Others watched with worry, mouths open, as the bewildered dog shook off the dizziness and tried rising to his feet.

The squirrel was long gone, so Rosco tried to free himself. But the wires—now loosened from the stakes—became twisted around his paws. The more he tried to get out, the more tangled he became. The whole effect was nothing short of pitiful.

"I told you all he ever does is get into trouble!" said Mason. "What a dumb dog!"

Several other kids burst into laughter.

"Rosco!" James frowned. "What are you doing? Get out of there, boy!"

But Rosco could not very easily do so. He wasn't hurt, but getting untangled was going to take a while.

"He's not dumb, Mason," said James. "It

was an accident." James was getting very tired of Mason's remarks about Rosco.

"I know, James. I was only kidding," said Mason. "It's just so funny! Seriously though, maybe you should go and get him out. He looks stuck."

The crowd of children watched as Rosco wrestled with the wires.

"Yeah, I'd better," said James. "Mr. Da Costa won't like the mess when he comes home from work today, either. But I'm not sure if there's enough time before the bus comes." He dropped his backpack and hurried down the sidewalk.

When James reached his dog, Rosco had just finished freeing his front legs. James unraveled the wires and pulled them off of his back legs. Rosco stepped out. "Be careful, boy, and go home now!" James pointed.

Rosco glanced toward the house and took a few steps in that direction—then stopped. He still had exploring left to do.

A moment later, the school bus rounded

the corner. *Oh, man.* "I have to go to school, Rosco. Go home and stay out of trouble—please!" James turned and headed back.

Rosco stood where he was, not moving, watching James go.

James reached the group, grabbed his backpack and stepped into line. He turned his head to look at Rosco as the other students filed onto the bus.

"Is he okay?" Mason asked.

"Yeah, I think so. I told him to go home, too. Hopefully, he'll listen," said James.

"I dunno." A girl from the fourth grade interrupted them as she climbed onto the bus. "I think that was a pretty dumb thing for a dog to do. Your dog's not very smart, is he?"

James shot her an angry look and stepped onto the bus.

"Look outside, you guys!" the girl called, taking her seat. "James' dog got all caught up in Christmas lights a few minutes ago! It was so funny!"

The other kids sat up and looked out the

window and laughed.

Last in line, James sank down into a seat and pulled his hood tightly over his head. But he peered out the window at Rosco, who still stood in the same spot.

"Looks like he'll manage, James," said Mason. "Don't worry."

"I hope so," said James. "But now the whole school's going to think my dog is totally idiotic. And they're all laughing at me."

"Who cares, James? Anyway, they're not laughing at you. They're laughing at Rosco."

"That's right—they're laughing at Rosco. And he's my dog, so that's the same as laughing at me," said James, lowering his voice again. "But that's not the point. You could've just kept your mouth shut in the first place, Mason. Why'd you have to announce it—why'd you have to call him dumb? Everyone heard you, and then they said it, too."

"Well, sorry, dude, but someone else

would've pointed it out if I hadn't said anything. Plus, Rosco isn't smart enough to know we were laughing at him."

"Yes, he is. He's very smart," said James.

"Doubt it," said Mason. "He's been making a mess of things all over town ever since we entered the contest. If he hasn't stopped getting into trouble by now, he's never going to. He has no clue that he should just leave all the Christmas decorations and lights alone."

James huffed.

"Anyway, we'll have to go and fix those lights after school before Mr. Da Costa gets home. We can't let him see what a mess old dumb-dumb Rosco made."

James sat up. "Aw, come on, Mason. Quit making fun of him."

"Quit getting so mad, James. I'm only kidding."

James sat back again. "Anyone's dog could've done that. It was a simple mistake. He was just chasing a squirrel, for crying out loud. All dogs chase squirrels."

"Exactly. Rosco is just as dumb as any other dog. It's not an insult." Mason straightened his shoulders and sat back against the seat.

"Yeah, it kind of is," said James.

"You don't have to be so sensitive, James," said Mason. "You sure don't sound like someone who wants help cleaning up today."

"That's because I *don't* want your help. I'll do it myself," said James.

"Fine," said Mason. "Go ahead."

"Fine. By the way, Mason, you've got Rosco all wrong," said James. "He's not dumb at all. You've never seen it happen, but he's saved us from trouble more than once or twice. He's really smart."

"Sure, he is," said Mason, with a sly smile. "I'll believe that when I see it."

James stared straight ahead. This whole thing was getting really old.

* * *

From the grassy lawn across the block, Rosco watched as the big, yellow bus pulled away. He hung his head low. He wasn't hurt, but he felt terrible just the same.

He'd heard the laughter. He knew he'd looked foolish.

Oh gosh, he thought. *I did it again. I let him down. I've got to stop letting James down.*

CHAPTER 7

FALLING APART
AT THE WHEELS

"Careful, Mom. Watch the elf hat," Mandy said. "Wait, I'll hold it." She grabbed it from her head, clutching it in one hand as they stood next to the minivan in the school parking lot. "Okay, ready."

Mom lifted the gingerbread train car over Mandy's head and slipped it down over her shoulders. Mandy settled her arms at her sides on the outside of the box.

"Okay, there you go." Mandy placed the cap back on her head. The children in her class had made elf hats at school yesterday and were allowed to wear them today if they wanted to.

Mandy raised one shoulder higher than the other, up and down a few times. Something didn't feel quite right.

"Honey, your straps are a little crooked, aren't they?" Mom said.

"Yeah, I guess they are. But it's okay. I'll be fine."

"Alright, then," said Mom. "Well, again, I like that can-do attitude, young lady."

"Thanks, Mom," Mandy headed onto the school grounds. "Bye!"

"Have fun! I'll be watching when you march by!" Mrs. McKendrick started across the parking lot toward a group of parents standing along the parade route.

Outside the classrooms, the children were lining up. Mandy glanced about. There were some pretty amazing train cars. She scanned the line of students as she made her way to the back of the line.

Her classmate Matthew was dressed like Santa on Christmas Eve, in a red suit and hat with a white beard. He stood inside his cardboard box, which was painted to look like the bricks on a chimney. Cotton balls lined the top of it like snow. "Ho ho ho!" he said. A few kids chuckled.

Another girl, also dressed in a red suit, carried a handmade cardboard sleigh on her shoulders attached by straps. A plastic reindeer had been fastened to the front. She held her head high as she shuffled by on her way to the first-grade line.

Wow! That looks amazing! Mandy swallowed hard and looked down at her gingerbread car. Her car wasn't nearly as detailed as some of the others.

Becca, also from Mandy's grade, had an enormous train car: a huge box wrapped in glossy gold paper and tied with fuzzy red ribbons. It was dazzling. Only Becca's head stuck out of the top of the box. Her long black hair was neatly tied with a big red bow on top. She looked like a walking Christmas present.

Wow! How did she think of that? I've never seen anything like it! Mandy looked down at her gingerbread car again and frowned.

A few seconds later a gumdrop broke off of her train car and fell to the floor. She reached down to pick it up, forgetting that she was standing inside of a stiff cardboard box. The giant lollipop wheels on the bottom of the box hit the ground with a small thud.

Uh-oh. She stood up straight, pulled an arm out from under her strap, and looked down. One of the wheels had cracked from the center of the wheel to the edge. The crack looked like a <u>spoke</u> on a bicycle wheel. Mandy bit her lip. *Oh no.* She reached down to check if the lollipop wheels were still glued on tightly. They were. *Whew. Maybe no one will notice.*

Joshua was in line ahead of Mandy. His car had been constructed out of several boxes and oddly shaped cartons to look like a shiny silver racecar.

Mandy's stomach tightened. *How in the world did he do that?*

"Mandy!" Trisha called from behind her, stepping in line. "I like your car!"

Mandy breathed a sigh of relief. "Hi Trisha! Thanks!" Trisha was Mandy's best friend. "I like yours, too!" Trisha's train car was decorated with dozens of flowing green ribbons to look like a pine tree. Colorful lights hung from it, shining brightly. Trisha wore a headband with a gold star on top. She looked like a Christmas tree.

"What do you think?" Trisha asked.

"I-I can't believe it!" Mandy stammered. "It looks so pretty! But—how did you ever come up with that?"

Trisha smiled and thanked her. "It was my mom's idea," she said, watching as more kids joined the line. "I helped her make it."

They waited in silence, watching the other kids line up. After a few minutes, a boy a few spots behind them stole an elf hat off of another boy. He sent it flying through the air, and soon, half a dozen second-grade boys tossed it from one boy to the next. They dodged left and right, attempting to catch the hat.

"Hey, guys, watch out!" said Trisha. "You're going to run into someone!"

The boys ignored Trisha and continued tossing the hat around. Its owner tried frantically to take it back. He was having no luck though, since his own train car made it difficult to move about quickly. Mandy looked desperately toward her teacher, who was involved in conversation with another child, hoping she'd say something.

But it was too late. One of the boys accidentally bumped into Trisha, who was caught off guard and bumped into Mandy. Before Mandy knew what was happening, she had lost her balance.

"Whoa!" Mandy cried.

Trisha wobbled, but she managed to grab Mandy by the arm just in time to stop her from falling over.

"Whew—close one!" said Mandy.

But just like that, the already-cracked lollipop wheel broke off entirely and hit the floor. The girls held their breath as the wheel rolled across the hallway like it was in slow motion.

The lollipop wheel smacked into the wall and broke into three big pieces.

"Oh no," whispered Mandy.

"Looks like your gingerbread house got a flat tire," Becca smirked. "Maybe you should call a tow truck." Her friends giggled.

"Not funny, Becca," Trisha scolded. "Leave her alone."

"Anyway," said Mandy, "trains don't have tires. They have wheels." Mandy raised her chin. "And it's not a house. It's a train car."

"Looks pretty bad *whatever* it is. Did a kindergartner make it for you?" Becca flipped her ponytail and turned back to face her friends. A giggle broke out among the group.

Trisha searched Mandy's face. Mandy had gone pale. "Mandy?"

Just then, a train whistle blew and *Jingle Bells* began to play over the loudspeaker.

"All aboard!" the principal shouted from the front of the line. "Let's march!" A cheer broke out across the line of students as they began moving forward.

But Mandy didn't feel like marching at all. In fact, she felt as though she were frozen in place. Her feet felt heavy and her train car even heavier.

"It's your turn, Mandy," said Trisha, nudging her gently from behind. "Go ahead. Everyone's walking."

Mandy wiped away a tear, hoping Trisha wouldn't see.

"Mandy, are you okay?"

Staring at the ground, Mandy lifted her feet and took a few steps.

Maybe it wasn't so bad. Maybe she could just ignore the fact that her train car was now missing a wheel, and that her classmates were laughing at her, and that one shoulder hurt from holding up the uneven straps. She took another few steps forward and exhaled deeply. *It's fine. I'm fine.*

Just then, the ribbon on her left shoulder broke free from the back of the box, and her train car lunged to one side. It hung there, lopsided across her back. Mandy stopped.

In a panic, she grabbed the ribbon, holding it tightly before the whole box fell to the ground. She moved forward again so she didn't fall behind the other students in line.

The box was heavy—how was she going to hold it up for the whole parade? Her left arm was already tired.

Why was this happening to her? Everyone else was having such a great time, smiling and waving at the crowd of parents, teachers, and students. They were smiling for photos and enjoying the Christmas carols over the loudspeaker.

But here she was, struggling to hold up her heavy, lopsided train car, hoping no one would notice the missing wheel and the lost gumdrops. She'd worked so hard. It was so unfair. She stared down at it. *A gingerbread car was a bad idea, wasn't it? And it's such a mess now!*

She sniffled and held back a sob. *That's it. I never should've done this by myself.*

Mandy wished she had listened to her

mother—if she had just let Mom use the glue gun for her, she would probably still have four wheels.

If she had just let Mom attach the ribbons, she probably wouldn't be stuck with crooked, broken straps. But it was too late now.

CHAPTER 8

FRUITCAKE

"Charlotte, you're next. Please spell the word *icicles*," said Miss Fitzgerald. "After a snowstorm, beautiful *icicles* hang from every tree."

"I-C-I-K-O-L-S," said Charlotte. "*Icicles*."

"I'm sorry, Charlotte. That's incorrect. The correct spelling is I-C-I-C-L-E-S." Charlotte pouted, walked to her desk, and slumped into her seat.

Twenty-three fifth graders were left standing side by side at the front of the classroom. Only two had returned to their desks after incorrectly spelling a word. James' class was competing in its regular

Wednesday spelling bee, which was Miss Fitzgerald's way of helping the students practice for Friday's weekly quizzes.

The class had just returned from watching the younger kids march in the Holiday Train Parade outside. James had seen his sister shuffle by. He was surprised that she didn't look happier—she'd been so excited this morning—but he couldn't get close enough to ask her if something was wrong.

The weekly spelling bee was one of James' favorite things about Miss Fitzgerald's class. He thought it might brighten up his dreary morning, after the <u>incident</u> at the bus stop.

He was good at spelling and he often won. This time, to add to the fun, Miss Fitzgerald used Christmas-themed words for the list.

"Ava, you're up. Can you spell *wrapping paper*? Children love to tear open the wrapping paper on their gifts."

Ava began. "W-R-A-P-P-I-N-G P-A-P-E-R. *Wrapping paper*."

"Very good," said Miss Fitzgerald. She turned to Henry.

"Henry, the word is *sleigh*. As in, 'Dashing through the snow,'" Miss Fitzgerald sang, " 'in a one-horse open *sleigh*.'"

A few kids giggled as Henry cleared his throat. "S-L-A-Y," said Henry. "A one-horse open *sleigh*."

"I'm sorry, but that's incorrect," said Miss Fitzgerald. "That's the other kind of *slay*, the kind with daggers or swords. The correct spelling here is S-L-E-I-G-H."

"Aw, man." Henry trudged back to his desk and slumped down into his chair.

"Leo, you're next. Can you spell the word *Noel* for us?" said Miss Fitzgerald. "As in, 'The First *Noel*, the angel did say...'"

"N-O-E-L," said Leo, straightening his shoulders. "*Noel*. Easy."

"Excellent," said Miss Fitzgerald. "Emily, you're up. Please spell *cheerfulness*. Peace, joy, and cheerfulness abound during the Christmas season."

Emily flashed her brightest smile and spelled the word.

On and on it went until most of the class was eliminated. Finally, only five students were left.

"Asher, please spell the word *chimney*. On Christmas Eve, Santa Claus comes down the *chimney*."

"That's easy. C-H-I-M-N-E-Y."

"Very good, Asher," said Miss Fitzgerald.

"Next, James, your word is *fruitcake*. My Aunt Melinda sends us a *fruitcake* in the mail every December." Several kids turned to each other to make funny faces and snicker.

Riley leaned over toward Asher. "My mom says it tastes like you're eating a brick with candy in it!"

"I hate fruitcake," whispered Asher.

Clara put a hand across her mouth and whispered to the students sitting near her. "If you're a fruitcake, it means you're a nut. You know—crazy, like this!" She stuck out her tongue, dug a finger into each ear, and looked at them googly-eyed. A wave of giggles broke out across the aisle.

"Settle down, fifth graders," said Miss Fitzgerald, disguising a grin. *Fruitcake* is a perfectly good word for Christmas, whether your Aunt Melinda sends you one or not." More laughs came from the class. "Now James, your word, please."

"Um, *fruitcake*," said James. "F-R-U-I-T-C-A-K-E."

"Very good. See, James knows all about fruitcake." More laughter erupted across the room.

James' cheeks turned bright red. *Oh, man.*

Miss Fitzgerald gave James an apologetic smile. "All right, class. That's enough. There's nothing wrong with a little fruitcake." The class erupted with laughter again.

The spelling bee was now down to only James, Stella, Ava, Mason, and Asher.

"Stella, your word is *reindeer*."

"Uh, can you use it in a sentence, please, Miss Fitzgerald?"

"Well, sure, Stella. If you need one." Miss Fitzgerald looked suspiciously at Stella, who seemed to be stalling for time. "Let's see. How about this? Eight tiny *reindeer* pull Santa's sleigh."

"Reindeer," Stella said. "R-E-I-N." She paused, counting out the letters on her fingers. "D-E-A-R. *Reindeer*. But actually, Miss Fitzgerald, they're not very tiny. And nine of them pull the sleigh. You forgot about Rudolph."

"That's true, Stella, you're right! There are nine. My mistake. But I'm very sorry. That is not the correct spelling of the word *reindeer*. It's R-E-I-N-D-E-E-R with two E's at the end. Please take a seat."

Stella's mouth flew open. She stomped back to her seat.

"Better luck next time. Ava, you're up. Your word is *anticipation*. Children are filled with *anticipation* throughout the month of December as they wait for the holidays to arrive."

"Awesome! I know this one!" said Ava. "*Anticipation.* A-N-T-I-S-I-P-A-T-I-O-N. *Anticipation.*"

"I'm sorry, Ava, but that's incorrect. It's a C, not an S in the middle of the word. It's A-N-T-I-C-I-P-A-T-I-O-N. Please take your seat."

Ava hung her head and sighed, and dragged her feet until she reached her seat.

"Wow, all the star spellers are dropping like flies now," Ian whispered to Leo.

"Mason, you're up. Your word is *cranberry*. Please pass the *cranberry* sauce," said Miss Fitzgerald.

"Easy. C-R-A-N-B-E-R-R-Y. *Cranberry*," said Mason.

"Very good, Mason."

"Asher, your word is *yuletide*. At Christmastime, we exchange *yuletide* greetings."

Asher's eyes went wide, as if he had never heard the word in his life. "Uh...Y-O-U-L-L." He took a deep breath then started again. "T-I-D-E."

"That is incorrect, Asher. I'm sorry. Please take your seat."

"Sorry, Miss Fitzgerald, but I never heard of a *yuletide*," said Asher. "Is that like a high tide?" The class giggled.

"It is nothing like a high tide," said Miss Fitzgerald, grinning. "Or a low tide, as a matter of fact. But, that's a good question. Asher, you may find a dictionary in the back and look up the word. When we're finished here, you can read us the definition. The correct spelling is Y-U-L-E-T-I-D-E."

"Hmmm," he said softly, raising an eyebrow before heading for the book stacks at the back of the room. "Okay."

Miss Fitzgerald glanced at her note cards and turned back to face the kids left standing at the front. "Mason, it looks like it's just between you and James now. Your word is *tinsel*. Here's your sentence: shiny silver *tinsel* can be used to decorate a holiday tree. Can you spell *tinsel*?"

"I think I can," said Mason, holding his head high. "T-I-N." He paused for a long moment. "S-E-L. *Tinsel*."

"Excellent. Looks like someone knows his holiday words," said Miss Fitzgerald. Mason beamed.

"James, you're up," she continued. "Your word is *poinsettia*. For Christmas, Mother decorates the table with a bright-red *poinsettia* flower in a pot."

James chewed on his lip, thinking. *Oh man. That's a hard one.* He cleared his throat.

"Um...*poinsettia*. P-O-I-N-T," James stopped, chewing his lip again. "S-E-T," he continued. The class was hushed, hanging on every letter. "T-I-A. *Poinsettia*."

Miss Fitzgerald gave James a kind look and frowned. "I'm very sorry, James. But that is incorrect."

84

"Really?" asked James, puzzled. He thought for sure he'd spelled it right.

"I'm afraid so," said Miss Fitzgerald.

James exhaled loudly through his nose as he took his seat. *Doggone-it.*

"Mason, you're the last one left," said Miss. Fitzgerald. "That means you must correctly spell the last misspelled word if you're to be our winner. Can you spell *poinsettia*?"

"I think so," said Mason. "P-O-I-N." He paused, eyes to the ceiling. "S-E-T-T-I-A. *Poinsettia.*"

"That is correct!" said Miss Fitzgerald. The class exploded with a round of applause.

James inhaled deeply and fixed a gaze on his desk, his cheeks growing hot. *I was only one letter off!*

"Excellent. Congratulations, Mason," said Miss Fitzgerald. "Class, you all did a great job today, but the top speller gets a prize!" The class continued to clap as Miss Fitzgerald handed Mason a candy cane that was twice the size of a pencil.

"Thanks!" said Mason.

James frowned as Mason returned to his seat, holding the candy cane high.

"Miss Fitzgerald," said Asher, raising his hand. "I found the definition of yuletide."

"Wonderful. Go ahead, Asher."

"Um, it says *yuletide: of or relating to the Christmas season.*" Asher grinned. "That makes a lot more sense than a high tide." The students erupted into laughter again.

James slammed his elbows on the desk and rested his chin on his hands, ignoring the fun. All Mason ever did was win, win, win. James could've spelled *cranberry* and *tinsel*, so why did he get such a hard word? Mason heard most of the correct spelling of *poinsettia* from him, anyway. If *he* had gone second on that word, he would've won. *It isn't fair! Why was this week turning out to be so bad?*

CHAPTER 9

MY BIG MOUTH

James climbed onto the bus after school. Mason followed and sat down next to him like nothing was wrong. But James was still angry.

"Mason, why'd you have to go and ask the guys to help us patrol on Friday? I don't need their help."

"I don't know. They sounded like they wanted to be involved."

"Well, why can't you at least ask me first before you open your big mouth?"

Mason huffed. "My *big mouth*? Last time I checked, it was my neighborhood. Why do I need your permission?"

"Because it's my neighborhood, too, not theirs! They didn't help us win the contest. They weren't out there stringing hundreds of wires onto the rafters or unpacking toy trains and snowmen all week. Why should they take all the glory and get to do all the cool stuff on opening night? That was our job. It's not fair."

"They're not taking any glory, James. They're just helping us keep an eye on things. They were going to be there anyway for the tour. What's the big deal?"

"I'll tell you what the big deal is, Mason." James' voice grew louder. "If you could just let someone else handle things for a change, and not take over—like you always do—this first-place win would be a lot more fun for the rest of us—mainly, me! My dad and I planned all of this!"

Mason breathed out through his nose. "I live there, too, James. Everyone on the block worked on it, including me, and *my* dad." Mason looked around at the other students. A few girls had begun to stare at them. "And take it down a notch, James. People can hear you."

James furrowed his eyebrows and glanced around the bus. He lowered his voice.

"You don't understand because things are so easy for you, Mason. You always win. Why couldn't you just let someone else have a turn this time?" James straightened his shoulders and faced the bus seat in front of him, a sour look filling his face. "Opening night was supposed to be my night. Now the guys think we only won because of you, because *you* always win."

Mason sat in silence for several seconds, took a deep breath, and let it out. "James, you win at stuff all the time, too. You're always head-to-head with me. Like the spelling bee today."

"Yeah, exactly like the spelling bee. I came in second place. I'm always second-best next to you."

Mason frowned.

James went on. "But this time I was number one. Sure, you and your dad did your house. But me and my dad—we made this *whole thing* happen. So I think it's only fair that I called the shots this time. Don't you?"

Mason sighed and stared out the window as James continued.

"But you couldn't help yourself, Mason, could you? You had to step in and take over." He turned back to face Mason. "Listen. Can't you just tell the guys we don't want their help? Can't you just uninvite them?"

"No, James! They're coming." Mason pounded his fists on his lap. "I want them there. They want to help! It'll be more fun anyway! I still don't see why you wouldn't want them there. They're your friends, too."

"Fine." James faced straight ahead. "Then I'll patrol my side of the neighborhood alone. You guys don't need me. You can do your own side of the block."

"Really?" Mason <u>gaped</u> at him. "You would do that—patrol alone? Take all the fun out of it just because you don't get to be top dog? Just because you're not in charge?"

"Yeah. I would do that. I don't need you, and I don't need the guys. I can do it alone."

"What will your dad say?"

"My dad won't say anything because he won't know." James was getting worked up again. "He only cares that we keep the block looking good. He won't care how we do it, so I'm not going to tell him. I wouldn't want him to know you turned it into a party, anyway."

"Fine, then," said Mason, rolling his eyes. "Go ahead. Have it your way. Patrol your side of the block *all by yourself.*"

"Fine. I will."

The bus slowed to a stop. Mason stood up. With another blank stare, he walked down the aisle, not looking back. "Later, dude."

Blood boiling, James exited the bus behind him and headed for home. "Humph."

CHAPTER 10

TROUBLE-STOPPER

"Hey, boy," said James, dropping his backpack on the floor. "How are ya?"

Rosco was lying at the foot of the staircase. Mom had covered the banister with pine branches, red ribbons, and holly, and a few of the pine needles had fallen on Rosco's back while he napped. James knelt down to pet Rosco and brushed off the needles. "It made me really mad when all those kids laughed at you today, boy. I'm sorry I couldn't stop them."

Rosco sat up and gazed intently as James stroked his soft ears. "But don't worry. I know you didn't mean to tear down the lights in the yard—you probably just got carried away. I know you're way smarter than that."

Raising his eyebrows, Rosco frowned like a sad puppy.

"I believe in you, buddy. I know you always mean the best, and I always tell them that. But the other kids think you're just a troublemaker."

James sighed. "So, do you think maybe you can start showing everyone that you're not? I just want them all to see the Rosco who's helpful and reliable and stuff—especially Mason."

Rosco settled back down to consider this. He had been right this morning—James *was* disappointed in him, and moreover, James was getting tired of making excuses for him.

Rosco didn't want to be thought of as untrustworthy or foolish. He would have to do better from now on.

Rosco nudged James with his snout. He wanted James to know he understood.

"Aw, thanks, boy." James relaxed. "Hey, guess what? I told Mason that I'm through working with him, and that I'll be doing block patrol on my own."

Rosco listened, his eyes filling with concern.

James fiddled with the holly leaves on the staircase. "Anyway, it's still gonna be really fun this weekend, Rosco. Doesn't matter if Mason and I aren't friends anymore. You're gonna be amazed when all the people come to see the lights and decorations on opening night."

James picked up a tennis ball that Rosco had left lying around. He bounced it off the floor, caught it, and bounced and caught it again as Rosco watched him. "It's only two days away. It's gonna be so cool, even if patrolling won't be the same as we planned."

Rosco felt sorry for James, and sorry for embarrassing him this morning. But his ears shot up. Wait—what was this about crowds of people coming to see the lights? *That's* what opening night meant?

James went on. "They'll see why we were voted the very best block. We'll show them we've got the best Christmas lights in town."

Rosco tilted his head to one side to listen more closely. He let out a soft whine. To

Rosco, James was finally starting to sound happy again.

"We'll show them we've got the best Christmas spirit, too!" James scratched Rosco behind the ears. "Won't we, boy? We'll spread Christmas cheer to everyone!"

So that's what we won? Rosco stood up and quickly shook off the guilty, sad thoughts. It was all starting to make sense. They were trying to spread the Christmas spirit. That's what they were *best at.*

He flashed his doggie smile and watched the ball bounce up and down, up and down.

"I've got to fix up Mr. Da Costa's lights now, Rosco. We aren't gonna look like the best block if even one yard is a mess. Be a good boy and stay here. I'll take care of it by myself. Here, go fetch!" James threw the ball down the hallway and Rosco chased after it.

Rosco ran fast. He would listen—he would stay put inside the house just as James instructed. As a matter of fact, he would be on his best behavior—at all times—from now on. He caught the ball and hurried to the window to watch James.

Finally, it all made sense. The displays outside were for making things merry and bright. They served a noble purpose—to spread Christmas joy. Rosco panted. He liked that.

He'd show the kids, especially Mason, that he was there to help. He'd stop being careless and clumsy. He'd stop being a troublemaker. He knew what he needed to do. He needed to be a *trouble-stopper*.

He'd be on the lookout for problems. If anything went wrong, if anything came along to put the Best Block at risk, he'd put a stop to it—immediately.

CHAPTER 11

CITY SIDEWALKS, BUSY SIDEWALKS

"James, I just want you to pour it. Can't you just do it?" Mandy begged. "It's really hot and I might spill it. Mom said you had to help me since she's helping Dad with the grownups."

"But you know how to do this," James insisted. "You've made hot chocolate before, and it's not *that* hot."

James glanced up the street. The first sightseers arrived by car. A steady stream of traffic followed the arrows and orange cones placed neatly along the streets. Other visitors began to park their cars outside of the tour zone and stroll the sidewalks. Soon, the block would be crammed with people.

Opening night of the Holiday Lights Tour had finally arrived and James and Mandy had set up shop in their driveway. The neighborhood was alive with color and sparkle. Bright lights twinkled to the sound of Christmas tunes roaring from several well-placed outdoor speakers. <u>Inflatable</u> snowmen swayed in the soft breeze and electric polar bears shimmered.

"Plus, Mandy, I've got to keep an eye on the neighborhood so you'll have to help pour. This hot chocolate stand was supposed to be your thing, after all."

Rosco gazed with excitement from the yard as lights blinked on and off in time to the music. *What an amazing sight!* He could hardly sit still.

"Well, it was mostly my idea, but you wanted to help, too, James. Don't act like you didn't."

James shrugged and set a paper cup on the countertop. "Fine, I'll pour it for now, but we better hurry up. Let's get ready in case we get a lot of customers all at once."

He poured hot chocolate from an oversized thermos into the paper cup. Mandy sprinkled marshmallows in and fastened a lid on top. "Perfect. Let's make each cup just like this when someone orders." He sipped it. "Yum."

Inside the house, Mr. and Mrs. McKendrick were busy with their party. Eight members of the city-planning committee who had judged the contest had arrived to check on the very Best Block and were enjoying the festivities in the meantime. Several neighbors had already stopped in, too.

James and Mandy were only to disturb them if they ran out of hot chocolate supplies or if Dad was needed to handle any mechanical problems with the lights or music outside. He'd attached his walkie-talkie to his belt in case James needed him.

Mandy turned to her brother. "James, how about if you talk to the customers and take their orders and what if *you* pour the hot chocolate like I already asked you, so I don't burn myself? And then maybe *you* take the money and make the change?"

James straightened his shoulders. "You

want me to do all of that? What are *you* going to do?"

"I'll do the marshmallows," Mandy said, lowering her voice, "and the lids. Like I just did. Please?"

James scratched his head. "What's gotten into you, Mandy? I thought you wanted to do all of this stuff." He replaced the lid on the thermos and twisted it tight. "You were so excited about it last week."

"Well, I did. But now I don't." Mandy turned away. She didn't want to tell James that the idea of running the stand without his help was making her sick with worry. Instead, she turned her attention nervously to the dozens of visitors streaming up and down the block.

In a yard several houses away, a few small children hopped around as lively Christmas music played. Noticing the hot chocolate stand, they tugged on their parents' coats, pointing and begging for some.

Mandy turned back to James. "Looks like

we might have our first customers soon."

"Good. But you can't just hide behind me, Mandy. You're going to have to take over the stand at some point because I have to go out on patrol. I can't do everything."

"I didn't say you had to do *everything*," said Mandy, pouting.

"Well, almost." James forced a half smile. "But, see the problem is that I'm in charge of every house around here. If something happens, I'll have to leave you for a while, so you'll have to handle it all at some point because I can't be in ten places at one time."

Mandy scrunched up her face. "What? Why would you have to be in ten places at one time?" But James ignored her question, still confused by her behavior.

"I don't get it," said James. "Why are you so afraid?"

"I don't know. I'll probably do it wrong, or break something, or something else bad will happen," said Mandy.

"What makes you think that? Nothing's

gonna go wrong. This isn't like you, Mandy. What's going on?"

Mandy opened her mouth to answer but froze. Across the street, a group of familiar second-grade girls walked down the sidewalk in the other direction, followed by a group of parents.

"Oh no! It's Becca and a bunch of other girls from school!" Mandy ducked below the counter. "I can't let her see me! What am I gonna do?"

"Who's Becca? Why can't you let her see you?" James looked down at his sister, huddled on the ground. Her face had gone pale. "Mandy, try not to freak out. Just tell me what's going on. Is she in your class?"

"No. She's not in my class, but she's in my grade. She made fun of my train car at the parade! James, go get Mom—please! I just don't think I can do this!"

"Slow down, Mandy," James bent down and placed a hand softly on her arm. "No one's going to make fun of anyone. You *can* pour hot liquid—without spilling it. I've seen you do it a million times. And Mom's too busy right now. Plus, I'm here, at least for now—we'll be fine without her."

"It's not that simple, James. Becca's mean. She ruined everything the other day at school—my train car almost fell apart, and she made fun of me for it. And then the other girls laughed, and I almost cried. So, if she laughs at me tonight, everyone will, and I'll probably cry this time. And then tonight will be ruined, too!"

"Slow down, Mandy," said James. "Wait—so *that's* why you weren't smiling when I saw you in the parade?"

"Yeah," she said.

"That stinks. I didn't know she did that." James stood up again and glanced at the group. "But don't worry," he said. "Those girls are walking in the other direction. Besides, there's nothing to laugh at. They'll *wish* this was their block—remember, we won *first place*? First place is pretty cool. And they'll wish that they could be running a hot chocolate stand like this."

Mandy twirled a lock of her long brown hair between her fingers, considering her brother's words.

"When they see you, *if* they see you tonight, since they might not even come back this way, they won't laugh at you. I know they won't."

"How do you know that, James? I'm not so sure. They'll still find a way to make me feel stupid, I bet." Mandy sighed heavily, peeking above the counter.

James thought about his week. Mandy did have a point. Mason had sure found a way to make him feel stupid. But he didn't want those kinds of things to happen to his sister. And he knew that if she could only start acting like her usual self, she wouldn't have a problem.

"Trust me, Mandy—you can handle this, even when I leave to go on patrol."

"I don't know about that, James. Just

please don't leave yet." She stood up from behind the stand and gazed across the street.

James watched the girls wander off, wishing he had as much confidence in his own situation as he did in Mandy's. "Don't worry. I won't."

CHAPTER 12

THE TIME HAS COME

A few minutes passed as more visitors strolled by. They stopped in front of each cheerfully decorated home to take photos or sing along to well-known carols playing on the sound system.

The tour was turning out to be a success, despite all the trouble this week. With a satisfied grin, James returned his attention to the hot chocolate stand.

"Mandy, I've got to go soon. But, here. I won't be needing this." He pulled the walkie-talkie out of his coat pocket and set it on the counter. "I don't even know why I brought it out here. You can have it since you'll be alone."

"What? What are you talking about?" Mandy eyed the device.

James shrugged, took out the change box to peek at the dollar bills and quarters inside, and nodded to the families walking by.

"Where's Mason, by the way?" asked Mandy.

"Mason's not coming. He won't be helping me. I mean—we're not patrolling together."

"You're not? But what happens if something goes wrong? Won't you have to radio each other so you can go fix it?"

"I can fix most things by myself, and I can patrol this end of the block on my own. Mason's going to patrol his own end of the block. He's got help now, anyway. He doesn't need me." James turned away. "I'll be fine. It's no big deal."

He glanced toward the house, where his bike sat leaning against the door to the garage.

"You mean, after all that planning, you're ditching Mason and doing this alone?"

"Yeah, well, I never planned on him being such a jerk."

"James, that's crazy," Mandy said. "At least take the walkie-talkie in case you need to radio Dad. This neighborhood is huge! Look at all these cars coming in! How will you ever be able to keep an eye on things all by yourself?"

James huffed and Mandy stopped for a moment, tapping a finger. "Oh...*now* I get it," said Mandy. "*That's* why you said you can't be in ten places at one time, because you actually might *have* to be."

James shot Mandy a disapproving glance but quickly recovered his smile as their first customers approached the stand.

Mandy picked up the walkie-talkie and slipped it back into her brother's jacket pocket. "Just hold on to it anyway, James. Dad will get mad if you lose it, and I don't want to spill hot chocolate all over it."

James frowned at her and cleared his throat. He didn't want to argue in front of strangers. "Okay."

As the customers ordered, Mandy set paper cups on the counter in front of James. James handed her the thermos and nodded at the cups. *You try*.

But she pushed it back with a silent plea. *I can't. You do it. Please?*

James shrugged and filled the cups with hot chocolate. Mandy topped them with marshmallows and lids and gently slid them in front of two children and their father.

When the man paid, Mandy thanked them. After they left, she said quietly, "Tonight *is* a big deal, James. This is not the time to start holding a grudge."

"You're absolutely right, sis'," said James, straightening his shoulders. "I should've started a long time ago." He grinned at her sarcastically and she gave him a tough look.

"But I don't understand. Why aren't you working together anymore?"

James explained what had happened. "After the other day with Mason, they all probably think I'm just a jealous nitwit who needs attention."

"Wow. That's a bummer, James. But how are you going to patrol this whole end of the block by yourself?"

"I don't know. It can't be *that* hard. I'll figure it out." James gazed at the lights that blinked up and down the street.

Mandy turned away, shaking her head slowly. "Okay, if you say so."

"Mandy, I can't be on a team with someone who acts like he does. I'm better off alone."

Mandy raised an eyebrow.

"Besides," said James, lowering his voice, "Mason makes fun of Rosco." He paused. "In front of everyone at school."

"What?" said Mandy, her voice growing louder. She placed a hand on her hip. "He does? Why would he do that?" She motioned at Rosco who sat pleasantly on the grass.

"Why would anyone do that?"

"I really don't know. He thinks Rosco's stupid."

Mandy frowned again.

"Anyway," said James, "I'd better start patrolling soon."

Mandy pouted. "Don't leave yet, James. I'm not ready. Stay longer. Please!"

* * *

Rosco listened with worry. Things were not going the way he had imagined. This did not sound like the way to spread Christmas cheer. Besides, he wasn't going to do anything silly or careless anymore, so Mason's teasing didn't bother him. He already had a plan to reclaim his solid reputation as a good dog.

James and Mandy don't need to worry about me. As a matter of fact, maybe I ought to worry about them.

Maybe he ought to start patrolling the area, just like James was planning to do. The time had come to be a trouble-stopper right here, right now, before things got any worse.

CHAPTER 13

COMET, CUPID, DONNER, & BLITZEN

The scene at the Best Block had grown quite lively. A steady stream of cars filled the streets while visitors filled the sidewalks.

A line of thirsty customers had formed in front of James' and Mandy's stand. Every now and then, Mrs. McKendrick hurried out of the house with refills of the <u>oversized</u> thermoses the kids were using then hurried back in to her guests.

"Thank you, sir," said James to the latest customer as Mandy set more cups on the counter. James had tried to leave on patrol but the line of customers had grown too long. He didn't want to leave Mandy alone yet—it was just too busy. "Enjoy your cocoa. Next!"

Rosco glanced about, on alert for any trouble. Not finding any, he returned his attention to the kids' hot chocolate business and all of the people in line. He'd keep an eye on them, just in case.

Next door, Sparks sat in the front

window, watching <u>contentedly</u> as the lights danced and the crowds strolled by.

A little while later, an eleven-year-old girl, a woman, and their puppies stopped on the sidewalk outside of Sparks' house.

"This looks like a good spot, Mom. Look at those cute little angel statues over there—they're perfect for *our* little angels." The girl pulled a cell phone out of her back pocket.

Sparks let out a playful bark when he saw four black-and-white Border collie puppies enjoying his yard.

Soon, Rosco heard cheerful, high-pitched yipping coming from Sparks' yard. He turned to look. *I wonder what's going on over there?* He trotted across his yard for a closer look.

"You're right, Sarah! This is a great spot." The woman knelt down and unfastened the leash from one puppy's collars. "Here we are, now. Stand still, Donner."

"Okay, boys," Sarah said to the puppies. "You all need to be on your very best behavior." She held up her phone and set it to camera mode. "Should we put them in front of the angels first, Mom, or maybe that gingerbread man over there? What do you think?"

"One second, Sarah. Let me finish with Comet and Blitzen." The woman unfastened the last leash and released the collies. "There you go, boys. Now, you can check things out with your brothers, but don't go far."

The woman turned back around and addressed her daughter. "Let's try both places. But watch it—you know how fast these little guys can be. Don't let them out of your sight for even a second."

"I won't! Oh, this is going to make the perfect Taylor Family Christmas card!" Sarah snapped pictures of Comet as he sniffed at the angels. "Wait until you see this one, Mom!" She held up her phone. "It's so cute!"

Excited to be free of the leash, Donner, Blitzen, and Cupid quickly romped across the yard, followed by Comet. It seemed that the

puppies did not care to stand still for a photo as much as they cared to inspect each and every object on the lawn.

"Oh, dear," said Mrs. Taylor. "This is going to be harder than we thought. How are we going to keep them together long enough to take a good picture?"

Sparks continued watching from the window, but he growled softly. The puppies were running circles around the large plastic reindeer statue in his yard. Their owners seemed to be losing control over them. They yipped gleefully, chasing each other's tails, but it looked like someone could get hurt.

Rosco also watched with growing concern. Still, none of the puppies noticed him. *Uh-oh. Looks like trouble.*

"Oh, my," said Mrs. Taylor, becoming more perplexed by the minute. "Maybe we'd better forget taking a picture and just catch them before they run away." She pointed. "You go there and I'll go here."

Mrs. Taylor and Sarah placed themselves at either end of the plastic reindeer. It didn't take long before Blitzen reversed directions, and Donner and Cupid smacked into one another, knocking the reindeer. All at once the reindeer <u>toppled</u> over, and all four puppies stopped, unhurt but dazed.

"Get them, honey!" said Mrs. Taylor, diving to the grass.

Oh boy. Rosco glanced at Sparks in the window and exchanged a knowing look with him. This was exactly the kind of thing Rosco had been worried about.

Sarah quickly captured a puppy. "I've got Donner!" But Donner wasn't ready to give up his freedom just yet. "It's okay, boy! Hold still!" But Donner soon broke free and ran from Sarah.

"Comet, Cupid, Blitzen—come back here, right this minute!" shouted Mrs. Taylor, starting after the collies.

Rosco's thoughts raced. This might be the perfect opportunity to rebuild his reputation. *I'll get these pups under control. No problem.*

He ran to the middle of the yard. "Ruff! Ruff!" he commanded. *Come back at once!* It was the kind of bark that his mother used when he was young, and it had always worked on him. "Ruff! Ruff!" *It's time to settle down, kids. Playtime is over.*

But the puppies didn't listen. Instead, they ran about even faster.

Sparks jumped from his place at the window and bolted to the kitchen, eager to help his pal.

Reaching his doggie door, Sparks scampered out. Mr. and Mrs. Benton probably wouldn't mind if he were gone for a bit. *Here I come, Rosco! I'll help you!*

But Rosco was struggling to understand why the puppies weren't listening to him. *I'd better tell them again.* He ran toward Cupid and barked in the puppy's face. "Ruff! Ruff!"

Cupid shrank back. His eyes grew wide. He zipped off in the other direction, glancing behind him to be sure the big, unfamiliar German shepherd wasn't coming after him. Just then, Sparks rounded the corner.

"Oh no!" said Mrs. Taylor. "Where did *those* dogs come from? They're scaring the puppies!"

"I think the little one came from inside this house. But I don't know where the big one came from," said Sarah, panicked. She continued to call. "Here, Comet! Here, Blitzen!" But every time she managed to close in on one of the puppies, it bolted away.

Mrs. Taylor <u>fared</u> no better. With Rosco and Sparks running circles after them, the puppies were just too scared to stay put. They zipped past her and into the yard next door.

CHAPTER 14

NOTHING UNDER CONTROL

Back at the hot chocolate stand, the line had shortened but remained steady. Mandy heard the <u>commotion</u> and watched in shock as the puppies ran by. She placed lids on two cups of hot chocolate and slid it in front of their customers. Plastering on a smile as James counted the change, she tried not to attract attention to the already <u>chaotic</u> scene.

"Thank you, ma'am. Have a nice night," said James.

With an anxious glance down the street, Mandy whispered to her brother. "James, are you seeing this?"

"Seeing what?" asked James, too busy to

notice what was happening next door.

"That." Mandy pointed, trying not to be obvious in front of the customers. James looked up just in time to see Rosco and Sparks running down the sidewalk in pursuit of several black-and-white puppies.

James forgot what he was doing and stared. He had the awful sensation of his heart dropping into his stomach. "You've got to be kidding me," he whispered. But he took a deep breath and turned to the next customer. "Uh, may I help you, sir?"

James' heart beat faster as he prepared another cup of cocoa. Of all the possible situations that he'd imagined on opening night, he never thought *Rosco* would start trouble.

"I'll go after them, Mandy. But try to act like nothing's happening, so we don't alarm these people. At least for now."

Oh man. James frowned, his thoughts racing. He should've started patrolling sooner. Maybe this never would've happened.

Or maybe it was worse than that. Maybe Mason had been right? Maybe Rosco *was* just a dumb dog.

James didn't know, and there was no time to worry about it. But one thing was for sure—it would soon be time for Mandy to run the hot chocolate stand by herself. Like it or not, he had to get going.

* * *

Further down the street, Sarah and Mrs. Taylor slowed to a walk as the dogs disappeared into the darkness ahead. "Gosh, Mom, are they going to hurt the puppies? That German shepherd is really big!"

Mrs. Taylor bent over, catching her breath. "He sure is! I don't think so, honey, but I sure hope not!" She lifted the pants around her ankle and inspected her foot, revealing fancy leather boots. "Oh, why did I have to wear these silly boots? I can't run in heels. My feet already hurt!"

"What are we going to do?" Sarah asked. "What if the puppies run out into the street?

They could get hit!"

"Oh goodness. Let's just hope they stay on the lawns. But there are lots of people about. Anyone would stop a helpless little puppy from running out into the street, right? Let's try and stay positive."

She glanced at the traffic and rubbed her gloved hands together vigorously, hoping she was right.

"I guess so," said Sarah. "But how are we ever going to catch them? How will we even find them? Can I go chase them by myself?"

"No, honey, I don't want us getting separated. Let's head in the direction they went."

Moving quickly, Sarah kept a speedy pace ahead of her mother. "I wish I could keep up with you, Sarah, but I just can't in these boots."

"Well, maybe we should go and get the car," said Sarah.

"I know we can't run as fast as anything on four legs, but we won't be able to catch them by car—that line of traffic is just too much! Come on. Let's just try on foot. We'll find them. But wait for me!"

* * *

Ahead, Rosco and Sparks sprinted after the collie pups, close on their heels. *Don't worry, Sparks, I've got this under control.*

Sparks eyed his friend suspiciously as he ran alongside him. Rosco, in fact, had nothing under control. "Ruff, ruff!" *Slow down, pups!* Rosco barked. But at the sound of his voice, the puppies began to scatter in different directions.

Rosco barked again, this time to his friend. *What's going on, Sparks? Why won't they listen to me?*

Sparks yipped. *Rosco, I think they're afraid of us—especially of you!*

What? Rosco slowed down, shocked. *Why would they be afraid of me? I wouldn't hurt a puppy!*

CHAPTER 15

ANOTHER ONE
OF HIS STUNTS

Sparks had figured correctly—Rosco had spooked the puppies. Rosco should have known that fierce barks from a big German shepherd like himself might scare them, but now it was too late.

Worse, the <u>chaos</u> created by two dogs in pursuit of four speedy puppies was quickly attracting the attention of more of their kind.

Soon, almost a dozen other barking dogs had ducked out of their yards and joined in on the chase.

* * *

"James, did you see that?" asked Mandy. "More dogs!"

James had just thanked a customer, and, for now, no other customers were waiting.

"Yes, I saw, all right. And I heard it." James shook his head. "I can't believe Rosco picked tonight to pull another one of his stunts! Why can't that dog just behave? Doesn't he know what other people think of him by now—what they already think of *us*?"

James thought for sure that Rosco had heard him the other day, had understood him on some level when he'd asked him to stop making mischief.

"I'm sure if he knew exactly what was going on, he wouldn't be doing this, James," said Mandy. "But he's just a dog, so take it easy. He doesn't understand *everything* we say."

They watched from a distance as two snowmen statues in a yard down the street toppled over. Barks and yipping noises sounded off as several strings of lights went out. Bystanders moved out of the way when one of the dogs ran off the grass and onto the sidewalk.

"Mandy, if word gets out that our dog started a <u>rampage</u> across the block, we'll be the <u>laughingstock</u> of Harmony. Plus, our entire neighborhood will be angry with us. Remember, there are contest judges right in there having eggnog and cookies with Mom and Dad." James pointed to the house. "Who knows what they might do if they see what's happening? What if they say we can't even be part of the tour anymore?" James was almost beside himself.

"James, calm down."

"Mandy, you and I both know what kind of trouble Rosco is capable of. So, please excuse me for thinking of the worst possible things!"

Mandy made a face. James wasn't wrong.

"Anyway," James continued. "I'd better go after him and fix the mess the dogs are making. We can't let the judges see what's happening."

Just then, they heard a clattering noise as

a stack of <u>oversized</u> <u>ornamental</u> gift boxes tumbled to the ground.

"Oh no!" said Mandy, wincing. "You're right. You better go now! I'll close the stand."

"Wait—what? Don't close the stand, Mandy! We've had a lot of customers and we'll probably have a lot more. Even if the lights tour is falling apart, at least the hot chocolate stand is going right. Don't give up now! You can run it by yourself."

"No—I can't!" said Mandy.

"Yes, you *can*. Anyway, Mom will be out with more hot chocolate soon. She can help."

"No, she can't! She told us she has to take care of the guests."

A group of kids and a woman were approaching, chattering about the pretty lights on the McKendrick's house.

"Well, Mom said Mrs. Benton was supposed to come out and help if it looked like we needed it. I saw her watching from her window earlier. She'll probably be out as soon as I leave."

Mandy took a deep breath and cast a doubtful gaze at her brother.

"Look, Mandy, you've got this. I know you do." James ran to the side of the house and jumped on his bike, waving as he pedaled away. "I'll be back soon!"

* * *

Further down the block, it was as though a small tornado made of dogs and puppies was sweeping across an open plain. The path of destruction grew by the minute.

As the dogs ran, they accidentally knocked over gingerbread men, turned over shepherd and herds of plastic sheep, and pulled strings of lights out of their sockets.

From behind, Sparks ran alongside Rosco. The two of them carefully avoided bumping into the decorations and lights. But Rosco's heart sank.

Oh, my goodness. I should've left well enough alone! I only made things worse by chasing the puppies, didn't I? The reality was all too clear.

Sparks yipped to agree with him.

But Rosco wasn't sure what else he could do now that the chase was on. "Ruff, ruff!" he barked. *Stop, everyone—please just stop!*

But none of them did.

CHAPTER 16

THREE TIMES
A FOOL

James pedaled fast, his anger growing.

Once was not enough. Twice was not enough. Three times now, Rosco had to make a fool of him and set everything into motion—crazy, out-of-control motion. When would this nonsense end?

More importantly, James thought, *how* would he stop Rosco? James rode down the street, careful to avoid the cars.

He squinted at the homes and yards ahead. Rosco and the dogs were nowhere in sight. James heard barking as he pedaled, and strings of lights in the distance went out every so often. If he had to fix all of this by himself, it would take all night.

How was he going to stop this mess from continuing across the entire neighborhood? He'd have to warn the neighbors on the other end.

James slowed his bicycle to a stop. A sinking feeling took over him as he watched a crowd gathering on a nearby lawn. What had happened?

A group of charming little elf statues had been arranged around a lifelike Mr. and Mrs. Claus. They all stood next to a street sign that was meant to look like it pointed to the North Pole. But the elves had been knocked down and lay this way and that.

The statue of Mrs. Claus lay face down on the ground, and the North Pole sign lay next to her. Even worse, every Christmas light on the house had gone out. It looked like no one was at home, either. The house and yard sat very still—silent, dark.

No Christmas joy here anymore. James sighed. This was bad.

James turned his gaze to the next house. Most of its lights were out and a large Christmas tree in the yard made entirely out of wires and lights was lying on its side—dark.

Oh, man. It's worse than I thought. The pack of big dogs must've come through here. Little puppies couldn't have done all that, right? He dropped his bike and ran across the grass, made his way through the crowd, and found his way to the display pieces.

James set Mrs. Claus back up on her artificial feet next to Santa. He pressed the signpost back into the ground and addressed the small crowd standing nearby. "Don't worry, folks—just a few dogs on the run. We'll handle it." As he returned the elves to an upright position, he tried to focus.

Maybe he should radio his dad—ask him to come out here and help set things up? It would be faster that way. Dad could even bring Mr. Da Costa or Mr. Benton.

James reached into his pocket and pulled

out the walkie-talkie.

But wait. What would his dad tell the judges? Or, what would they say if his dad suddenly left the party? Even if he told the judges nothing, surely they'd start asking questions. And then what?

James couldn't let that happen. He had to do something now, before things got even worse.

But he'd been too confident in his abilities—he couldn't clean up the mess that might span six whole blocks *and* stop the dogs by himself! Sixty houses were involved in the Best Block contest, and too much damage had already been done. He had to get help—fast.

James took a deep breath. He knew of only one person who wasn't busy with a hot chocolate stand or hosting a party—one person who was already out on patrol, like he was. One person who would be ready and willing to help him save opening night. *Four people, actually.*

James pushed the button.

"Are you there, guys?" said James. "Pick up, Mason. Over."

* * *

"Mason, here. What's going on, James? I thought you weren't talking to us anymore," Mason said with a casual glance at his friends. "Say hi, guys." He held out the walkie-talkie so the boys could say hello.

"Hey guys, look," said James. "I know I said I didn't need your help. But I—I do. Something's happened."

A look of surprise came over Mason's face. "What do you mean, James? What's going on?"

James' stomach turned a flip. "Um, I wish I didn't have to say this, but well—uh, it's Rosco. He's out of control. He decided to chase a pack of four little collie puppies—I have no idea why—and then a bunch more

dogs started chasing them, and now they're running around the neighborhood like crazy."

"No way!" said Mason. "Seriously? I knew it! I knew that dog of yours would do something like this. Didn't I say he would?" Mason high-fived Leo. He smiled, satisfied.

"Yeah, Mason. You did," said James,

sighing. "You were right. I should've known Rosco would do something like this. Over."

"Copy that, dude. No big deal."

"Thanks." James lightened his tone. "But listen—this is nothing to laugh about. The dogs are out of control. Lights and stuff are down all over the place. They're headed toward your side. They could destroy the whole block, which means we might lose our winning status."

The other boys listened closely and Mason grew serious again. "Uh-oh."

"We need to stop them, as soon as possible," said James. "For starters, we need to catch Rosco and the puppies. Do you think you guys can do that? I'll fix what I can down here and then come and find you. If you see the big dogs, try to catch them, too. Over."

The boys nodded, eager to help. "Copy that, James," said Mason. "We've got this. See you in a while. Over."

"Thanks, guys. Over and out." James breathed a small sigh of relief.

Well, I guess that could've been worse. He tucked the walkie-talkie back inside his jacket and got onto his bike.

CHAPTER 17

MEANWHILE, BACK AT THE STAND

"Fa la la la la" blared from the speakers as Mandy greeted the approaching customers. Her stomach turned somersaults. *You can do this,* she told herself, forcing a smile. *It's no big deal.*

"Hi. Four, please," said the woman, pulling out her wallet. Mandy lifted the thermos and carefully poured hot chocolate into three of the four paper cups she had set on the counter. But her nerves were working against her. Still shaking, she knocked over the fourth cup, and hot cocoa gushed onto the counter.

"Oh, no!" said Mandy as it spilled onto

the sidewalk. She tried to stop it with her hands. "Ouch! It's so hot! Oh, I'm so sorry, ma'am!"

The woman grabbed some napkins and began to sop up the mess. "It's okay, honey!"

Mandy swallowed hard. *I wish Mom were here.* When the counter was clean, Mandy apologized again. Her cheeks had turned bright red. "I won't charge you for those drinks, ma'am. I'm not usually so clumsy."

"Thank you, dear. But I insist. It was just an accident, and I'm used to spills around the house." She smiled and glanced at the three young children behind her then turned back to Mandy. "Are your hands okay?"

Mandy told her they were, and then she told herself to stay calm. She finished placing marshmallows in the cups and snapped on the lids. The woman was very patient. Thank goodness for that, thought Mandy.

A teenager waiting in the long line called out. "Hey, what's taking so long?"

Mandy glanced at the boy, then back at her house, desperate for a glimpse of her mother. Mom had checked on them earlier when things were going smoothly.

"Remember, I'm right inside if you need me, kids," she'd said. But right now Mom was nowhere to be seen and there were too many customers for her to go find Mom. Mandy just wanted to run and hide.

"Uh..." Mandy turned back to the friendly woman, eager to hurry things along. "Um, here's your last drink." She handed it across the counter and the woman gave Mandy some cash. "Thanks again, ma'am."

"Can we get on with this?" said another teenager from the line. "I don't have all night." An older couple in line glared at the teens with disapproval.

"Come on, guys, let's go." The teens left the line, scoffing at Mandy as they passed the stand. "This is taking way too long."

Please, Mom, where are you? Tears began to well up in the corners of Mandy's eyes for the second time that week. She really wished she had kept that walkie-talkie like James had offered. She could've radioed Dad and asked him or Mom to come outside and help.

"Why, hello there, Mandy! Your mother called and said you were out here all alone." It was Mrs. Benton, the friendly grandmother from next door who owned Sparks. "Your mother is too busy with her guests to come out, herself. Do you need a little help?"

Mandy let out a big breath and relaxed. "I sure do, Mrs. Benton. "Boy am I glad to see you! James was helping but he had to go out on patrol. And now the line is so long."

"Don't you worry a bit. Long lines mean business is hoppin'!" Mrs. Benton turned to the next customer. "How may I help you, sir?"

Within a few minutes, the line was moving along quickly. Mrs. Benton was really good at this, and Mandy felt like she was finally getting the hang of it. Running the stand was actually starting to be fun, even though she accidentally spilled a little bit of cocoa now and then.

"It looks like we're almost out, Mandy." Mrs. Benton took one of the large thermos containers from the counter. "I'll run inside and help your mother with a refill. Do you think you can handle things while I'm gone?"

Mandy glanced at the line, which had been fairly long all evening. But her confidence was back since her customers were leaving happy. "No problem. I'll be fine as long as I don't run out."

"Okay then. I'll be right back." Mrs. Benton hurried off.

Mandy grinned at her latest customer, "Thank you, sir. Goodbye!" But as he stepped aside, Mandy felt her stomach drop to the floor. Behind him, there stood Becca and her friends. Becca's mother and a few of the other girls' parents stood behind them, chatting with one another.

Equally shocked, Becca stared and then

blinked. Her face had gone pale. "Uh...hi, Mandy."

Mandy stood frozen. A couple of seconds passed before she could make herself say, "Hi Becca."

Finally, Becca tossed her head to flip back her long ponytail. She glanced at her friends and her usual smile returned. "Oh, my gosh, Mandy! You're working here?"

Mandy wasn't quite sure what to make of the question. The answer was obvious, of course, but was Becca impressed, or was she just looking for a way to make fun of Mandy again?

Mandy blushed, straightened her shoulders, and forced herself to speak. "Uh, yes. This is my hot chocolate stand—my brother's and mine. He's not here right now. I've been selling hot chocolate all night. Would you like some?"

"Oh. Wow," said Becca, stunned again. "You mean, you're running it alone?" She looked Mandy up and down, and Mandy really began to regret spilling hot chocolate down the front of her jacket earlier.

"Yes," Mandy said. "This is my house. My mom's inside making the hot cocoa for us while we—I mean, while *I* run the stand. My brother's out checking on the Christmas lights, so I've been running it by myself, mostly. My neighbor is helping me, too."

"Really? Wow. So *your* house is on the Best Block, then? It looks nice! And that's so cool! Isn't that cool, you guys?" The girls nodded eagerly.

"Uh, thanks," Mandy could hardly blink. "Uh, so, how many hot chocolates would you like?"

"Four, please," said Becca.

Mandy poured each drink without spilling a drop and sprinkled them with mini marshmallows. When she set the lids on the counter, Becca helped Mandy snap them on the cups.

Stepping forward, Becca's mother handed Mandy a five-dollar bill. "Keep the change, sweetie."

"Thank you very much, Mrs. Carlson." Becca's mom had tipped her a whole dollar. She hadn't had many tips tonight. Mandy appreciated it.

"You're very welcome, Mandy. I admire your hard work. Keep it up!" Mrs. Carlson and the other girls left the line and joined the other parents who were waiting for them outside the next house.

Becca stayed back. "I always wanted to run a lemonade stand," she said. "Or a hot chocolate stand. Your neighborhood looks so nice, Mandy. Congratulations on winning."

Mandy blushed again, hardly able to believe Becca could be so nice. With a cautious smile, she placed the money in the metal box and clamped the lid shut. Maybe Becca and her friends weren't so bad—just maybe.

"So, anyway, thanks, Mandy." Becca took a sip of the drink. "And—uh—also..." She glanced at the ground. "I'm sorry about the other day. Your train car was pretty cool. I could tell you made it yourself. I wouldn't even know how to do that."

"Oh!" said Mandy with a gasp. "Thanks! And, uh, that's okay."

"Thanks. See you at school," said Becca, turning to leave. "Merry Christmas, Mandy!"

"Merry Christmas," said Mandy, still <u>astonished</u>. Well, of all things, she certainly hadn't been expecting *that*.

CHAPTER 18

SLEIGHS, TRAINS AND PUPPIES, OH MY!

Somewhere in the middle of the neighborhood, Sarah and Mrs. Taylor hurried along the sidewalk.

"Mom, we haven't seen them *forever*. I wonder if they're already heading back the other way?" Sarah was at least three yards ahead of her mother.

"Honey, would you please slow down? This doggone heel is giving me so much trouble." Mrs. Taylor glanced at her high-heeled boots with an angry sigh.

"But Mom, we're never going to find them like this." Sarah was getting desperate and slowed only a little. "I mean, seriously, how are we *ever* going to find them?"

"We'll find them, honey. Don't worry. Let's keep looking."

But Sarah was not convinced. She finally stopped and turned to look at her mother. Tears welled up in her eyes and her voice went higher. "It's been too long, Mom! Can't we just go and get the car now?"

"Oh, sweetie, please don't cry! And yes, we can try that now. Oh, what a terrible week for your dad to be out of town! He could've helped us search."

Just then Mrs. Taylor heard a crack and a rip from her left boot. She stopped and lifted her foot to take a look. The heel dangled from the boot, broken partway. "Oh, my!" Mrs. Taylor looked nearly defeated. "I guess these boots just weren't made for walking."

Sarah wiped a tear from her cheek. "Are you all right, Mom?"

Mrs. Taylor stooped down for a closer look. With a quick snap, she broke the heel off completely and stuck it in her coat pocket.

In a dry tone of voice, she answered. "I am now." She stood up and started off again, this time limping from the uneven heels. "Come on, honey. It's time to get the car."

* * *

Elsewhere on the Best Block, Rosco and Sparks raced around decorations and strings of lights, trying their best to avoid the obstacles. They had lost track of the puppies as the little collies scattered into various yards, terrified of the big dogs.

I have an idea, Sparks! Rosco barked. *Why don't you run up there in front of the other dogs? See if you can get them to follow you into another part of the neighborhood? Maybe that'll keep them off the Best Block.*

Sure! Sparks yelped. *I'll try!*

Rosco slowed just enough to let him pass. *I'll go find the puppies and catch up with you later! Good luck!*

"Ruff! Ruff!" *Great idea, Rosco!* Sparks picked up speed until he reached the front of the pack. With a spirited little Pug as their leader, a new game of chase began, and the pack of dogs followed Sparks. He led them across a front yard and into a backyard away from the Christmas lights.

Good job, buddy. Rosco hurried down the block.

* * *

On the other side of the Best Block, Ian shouted to the other boys. "There goes a puppy!" It was Cupid, and the little dog ducked beneath a row of hedges that blinked with white lights. "I'll get him!" Ian dove to the grass.

He reached under the bush, feeling around for the dog, and found nothing but cold dirt. Just as quickly as Cupid had disappeared into it, the collie emerged on the other side of the bush, yelped, and dashed off. Ian scowled and brushed the dirt from his hands.

"There he goes!" cried Mason. The boys charged down the sidewalk.

In moments, they saw a gingerbread

house as large as a child's playhouse. It had gumdrops and peppermints the size of grapefruits, and fake snow painted on its roof.

"I'll bet he went in there!" Leo followed the path to the little house and ducked down to enter.

Inside the house, instead of Cupid, Comet lay on the ground, panting hard. Leo reached down and petted the dog softly on the head. "Hey, boy, don't be scared. I'm here to take you back to your owners." He picked up the puppy and tucked him inside his jacket.

Next door, Rosco trotted up. "Ruff, ruff!" he barked, spotting one of the pups on top of a life-sized red sleigh stacked high with wrapped boxes. *Come down from there this minute!*

"Hey, it's Rosco!" said Mason. "Let's get him."

Rosco stopped. He looked at Mason, a bit surprised to hear him say such a thing. Rosco

was here to help! But he was more concerned about the puppy and ignored the comment. "Ruff, ruff!"

Ian turned. "Wait, look up there, Mason—Rosco's barking at another puppy!"

he hollered. "I think it's the one that got away earlier!"

It was. Cupid stumbled about on the stack, giddy at having climbed up so high. He knocked fake presents off the sleigh as he pranced about. "Ruff, ruff!" the little dog yipped. *This is fun!*

"Ruff, ruff!" Rosco barked at Cupid. *Be careful! That's dangerous!*

But Cupid wasn't worried until the box he stood on tilted sideways. As it slipped free of the others, Cupid slid down the stack of presents while riding high on the box, as if on a sled.

Rosco froze, and the boys held their breath.

But just as quickly as he rode down, Cupid tumbled safely onto the grass and scrambled to his feet.

"Whew!" said Ian.

Rosco ran toward Cupid, barking. *Are you okay?*

But Cupid was still afraid of Rosco, and

the puppy dodged between the runners of the sleigh to hide.

"Get him!" Asher called, running to the front. Ian hurried to the back of the sleigh, leaving Cupid with nowhere to go. Ian reached under the sleigh and quickly grabbed hold of him. "Gotcha!"

Rosco looked on, satisfied. With only two puppies left to catch, this was going well. *Mason and the boys are very helpful, indeed.* He trotted up the sidewalk ahead of the boys, eager to find the last two puppies.

"Wait, Rosco! Come back!" shouted Mason.

Rosco turned to listen, but there was no time to waste. *I've got to find those other puppies, Mason. I'll see you soon.* He took off down the street at a run.

Before long, he heard the sound of a train whistle. *What could that be?* Rosco dodged several visitors strolling through the Holiday Lights Tour and rounded a corner. Another puppy appeared.

It was Donner. The puppy had found a battery-powered, child-sized train display that was chugging its way around a miniature track. The track encircled a well-lit Christmas tree. Large plastic presents sat beneath it, lit up with red and green lights. Donner raced around the track, chasing after the caboose like it was a game.

Kids! Rosco thought, smiling. *Ah, well, at least he's not hurting anything. I'll let him keep at it until the boys show up. They'll grab him. Looks like he's having fun.*

"I see another puppy—over there!" called Mason, rounding the corner. "He's on the train track. Come on, guys! And look, Rosco's there, too! Get them!"

Just then, Donner tripped on the track, toppling forward into a somersault. He lay there for a moment, surprised, and then returned to his feet. But by that time, the little train had nearly made its way around the circle once more and quickly caught up to Donner. Now, the puppy no longer chased the

train—the train chased the puppy!

"Ruff!" Rosco barked and stopped wagging his tail. *Get off the track, kid!*

But Donner was too scared to think clearly. So he ran around and around with the train closing in on him.

Silly boy—what's he doing? Why doesn't he jump off the track? He's going to get hit!

Rosco had to do something—fast.

"Ruff, ruff!" Rosco barked, racing alongside Donner on the grass around the track. *Jump, buddy! Jump off the track! You can do it!*

But Donner couldn't do it. He was simply too scared. *I guess there's only one thing left to do,* thought Rosco.

He moved in close to the track and waited. As Donner raced by, Rosco reached out and grabbed him by the scruff of his neck, then pulled back. In the next instant, the toy train charged by. *Toot, toot!*

CHAPTER 19

JOYFUL, JOYFUL

Rosco set Donner gently on the grass and licked his head. The puppy panted and rolled onto his side, worn out.

"Wow! Did you see that?" said Asher, hurrying over to the dogs.

Mason's eyes were wide. "I sure did."

"James' dog saved the little guy!" said Asher, patting Rosco on the back. "Good boy, Rosco! And you're a good boy, too," he said to Donner, petting his soft head. "But you'd better be faster next time you try to outrun a train." Asher laughed and scooped the exhausted puppy safely into his arms. "Much faster."

Mason grinned. "Seriously, though, I can't believe it. I never thought I'd see Rosco make an emergency rescue—of any kind."

Excellent, thought Rosco. *They're starting to see me as a trouble-stopper.*

From a block behind, James pedaled toward his friends. He had been all over the neighborhood, reconnecting panels of lights and fixing decorations that the pack of big dogs had brought down. It seemed like a good time to catch up to the guys.

James saw the boys up ahead and began pedaling faster. Suddenly, Sparks and the pack of escaped dogs emerged from the backyard of the house he had just passed. "Look out!" he hollered to his friends, trying to be heard over the Christmas music on the outdoor speakers.

The dogs had circled back from the other side of the neighborhood. Headed straight toward the boys from behind, it only took moments until they reached Leo.

Leo still clutched Comet in his arms. But

Comet didn't like the bouncing motion that happened when Leo hurried along, so Leo walked more slowly and had fallen behind the other boys. When the pack came upon him, Leo quickly dodged behind a tree to avoid being hit.

Whew. James kept pedaling past Leo and waved.

Leo signaled to James. *Thanks for the warning!*

Still leading the pack, Sparks carefully chose his path to avoid the decorations, hoping the pack would do the same. But they didn't. They ran recklessly into anything that stood in their way, breaking things at every turn.

James pedaled toward Mason and Asher. "Guys, watch out!" he called from behind.

The boys looked back to see the pack of dogs racing toward them at breakneck speed. But directly in their path was an electric lawn sign that read JOYFUL in <u>oversized</u>, lit up capital letters.

James <u>cringed</u>. "Oh no!" In just a few seconds, three of the dogs knocked it onto the grass and jumped over it, continuing forward. Its lights went dark.

"Aw man!" yelled James.

But it wasn't over yet.

A large, sturdy Rottweiler <u>barreled</u> across the lawn straight toward the guys. Still holding Donner, Asher stepped out of the way just in time.

But Mason had nowhere to go. The dog was approaching on his right, but on his left, several large round Christmas ornaments blocked any sort of quick escape there might be.

Mason hesitated, and in seconds, the Rottweiler smacked into Mason's legs, head-on. Mason <u>buckled</u> and collapsed onto the ground. The big dog stumbled and yelped, then picked himself up and kept running.

Behind the Rottweiler, a large Boxer, a tiny Pomeranian, a tall Labradoodle, and half a dozen more dogs appeared. Still on the ground, Mason rolled over on the frosty grass and shielded his head with his hands. Asher and Rosco could hardly bear to watch. When the last of the dogs ran by without hitting Mason, they hurried over. "Are you okay, Mase?"

Mason rolled back over, sat up slowly, and rubbed his leg. "Uh, I think so. He hit me hard."

"Here, take my hand. See if you can stand up."

Shaken, Mason grabbed Asher's hand and pulled himself to his feet. "Ouch," he uttered. "Thanks, Ash."

James pedaled up and braked as Mason dusted himself off. "You okay, Mason?"

"Yeah. Kind of." Mason winced, bending his leg. "Maybe a couple bruises. My knee hurts but I think it's okay."

"Sure wasn't anything *joyful* about that," Asher joked, pointing to the knocked-over sign.

Mason stretched his ankle. "You're not

wrong, Asher."

James glanced at the JOYFUL sign and put his bike on the grass. "I'll go see if I can get it working again."

Mason nodded. "Wait, James. I'll go fix the sign in a few minutes. It'll give me a chance to rest my leg. You and Asher should go look for the last puppy. I can't walk that fast, at least for now. Oh, and take Rosco. He's been really helpful."

A look of surprise crossed James' face. *Mason thinks Rosco is helpful now?*

"Okay, that sounds like a good plan, Mason." James eyed Mason curiously. "Why don't you take my bike so you don't have to walk when you're done?" asked James.

"Okay, good idea, James. Thanks. I'll catch up soon." Mason headed back to fix the sign, limping slightly.

* * *

Before long, Sparks left his spot at the front of the pack and circled back to explain himself. "Ruff, ruff!" he barked. *I'm sorry,*

*Rosco, but I can't stop them! I've tried
everything. It's as though they can't even
stop themselves. They just keep running. I
don't know what else to do!*

"Ruff, ruff!" barked Rosco. *Just stay with
them, Sparks, and try to guide them away
from the Christmas decorations and lights,
just as you've been doing. We'll help you
soon!*

Sparks yipped in response and sped off.

* * *

"We've got to stop those dogs!" said
James. "These puppies did nothing compared
to the trouble the big dogs are causing."

"I know! But how are we ever going to do
that?" Asher asked.

"I don't know yet," said James. "But I'll
come up with something."

Asher looked in the direction the pack
had run. "There must be at least twelve of
them now, maybe more, and they're so fast!"

"You can say that again," said James. He
sighed.

"Okay—they're so fast!" said Asher.

James laughed and returned a goofy look. "I meant—"

"I know what you meant, James. Just keeping it light."

James laughed again. "Good. I'm glad *someone* is."

Donner began to whine in Asher's arms. Asher pulled him closer and stroked his ears. "It's okay, buddy. Don't worry. We'll figure it out."

"Guys!" Suddenly Leo hurried toward them from behind. He caught his breath as he reached his friends. "Look!" He pointed.

From far off, the black-and-white fur was difficult to make out in the dim light. But the boys realized quickly what they were looking at. "Come on!" called James. "The fourth one—it must be!"

Indeed, it was. Blitzen was playing in the <u>festive</u> yard two houses over. The yard looked like a scene from a Christmas ballet, with sugar plum fairies and large wooden nutcrackers assembled across the lawn. Giant, lit-up, artificial snowflakes dangled on strings from the branches of the leafless tall trees. The whole effect was magical and when the boys reached it, they stopped in their tracks.

"Wow!" said Ian.

"I hadn't seen this one lit up at night yet." James gazed at the display. "It's amazing!"

"Uh-oh!" said Asher, turning and pointing behind them. "Guys, I think we have a problem. Look back there!"

The big dogs were back, and they were headed straight for the nutcracker yard where Blitzen played. Sparks was at the front again but he hadn't seen the fourth puppy in the yard. He thought he could lead them straight across the lawn while avoiding the decorations, which were spread out enough for a pack of dogs to run by and avoid. He thought he was directing the pack away from trouble, at least as much as possible.

"Sparks—wait! Not that yard!" Asher

called. But Sparks didn't hear him.

James was the only one left not holding a collie. "The puppy's going to get hurt! I'll go!" He took off at top speed.

Rosco raced ahead of James toward the pack, determined to help. But as the big dogs closed in on the yard, it made no difference. Rosco came upon the pack from behind and could do nothing to send the dogs in a different direction. Nor did the dogs try and avoid the decorations.

To everyone's surprise, tiny Blitzen jumped into action. With a quick, panicked bark, he raced toward a life-sized toy soldier guarding the walkway. Blitzen stopped and crouched at the enormous soldier's feet. Then he squeezed his eyes shut and buried his head in his paws.

"Border collies are really smart!" cried Asher. "He probably thinks the soldier can protect him!"

"Yeah, but it can't!" said Leo. "That's not a safe place for him at all! It's going to fall!

He's too young to understand!"

James watched with dismay as he ran, helpless to stop the pack.

As the evening wore on, only a few visitors were left at this end of the Best Block. They hurried out of the way as the pack swept by. Fairies, nutcrackers, and candy canes struck the ground as strings of lights went dark. Sparks was the only dog that bothered to avoid the decorations entirely.

With a few accidental heavy whacks from long tails and sturdy shoulders, the giant toy soldier wobbled. It swayed from side to side then plunged, face first. With a powerful smack, it hit the ground.

Blitzen lay beneath.

CHAPTER 20

GET HIM OUT!

The boys gasped. Terrified, they sprinted toward the scene. But the pack of dogs ran away until they disappeared from view. Sparks didn't even realize the other dogs had knocked over the large toy soldier.

Rosco reached the yard first and sniffed wildly around the soldier. "Ruff, ruff!" he barked.

Blitzen was pinned under the heavy wooden soldier, but the soldier hadn't hit him directly. Maybe it was pure luck, Rosco thought, but the puppy had been standing in the only possible spot that prevented him from being flattened. When the soldier hit the ground face first, the small drum that stuck out at the soldier's waist created an opening, and that was exactly where the puppy was caught. "Ruff, ruff!" *You're alive!*

"Arf, arf!" the puppy squeaked. He didn't like being stuck. *Help!*

Rosco pushed his snout into the open space, attempting to nuzzle Blitzen with the tip of his wet nose. *Don't worry—we'll get you out!*

Mason pedaled up and stopped next to two women with babies in strollers who had come over to see if they could help. Mason set the bike on the grass.

"Is he okay, boys?" one of the women asked. James glanced at them.

"I think so, but he's trapped. But don't worry. We'll get him out."

Mason walked with a slight limp. "What can I do, James?"

James crouched down and attempted to lift the heavy soldier. He could only raise one end, but that wasn't going to do any good.

"We've got to lift both sides at once. Can you get the other end, Mase?"

"Sure."

Together James and Mason slowly lifted the soldier off of Blitzen and returned it to an <u>upright</u> position. Blitzen scrambled out. He was unhurt but frightened and immediately broke into a run.

After a quick chase, Mason captured the puppy and lifted him into his arms. "Oh, you poor thing! Don't worry. I've got you now." Then he said to the boys, "Oh, he's so cute! This one's mine!"

"He's all yours, Mason," said James. "Now we've all got a buddy. I've got mine right here." James reached down and scratched Rosco behind the ears.

Mason nudged the tip of Blitzen's nose with his own. "I wish we could keep them!"

The boys began to put the yard back the way it had looked prior to the dog <u>rampage</u>.

"James," Mason said, setting <u>upright</u> a sugarplum fairy decoration that had fallen onto the grass. "I honestly can't believe I'm saying this, but Rosco has been helping us at every turn. I'm beginning to think that he didn't start this trouble on purpose, because every time he got near the puppies tonight, they ran away from him, even when we *knew* he was trying to help. I think they probably just got scared of him in the first place and ran off."

James listened.

Mason stopped working to pet Blitzen, who sat cradled in one arm. "Then, well, the other dogs must've started chasing Rosco and the puppies and everything went crazy after that."

James nodded. He wasn't actually surprised to hear that he'd been wrong about Rosco. He knew Rosco had it in him, and it had become obvious that Rosco was proving himself a hero tonight.

But he hadn't expected Mason to think so. Had Mason totally changed his mind? "You mean you don't think he's just a dumb dog, anymore, Mason?"

Mason shook his head. "Not at all. He's no dummy. Rosco is full of surprises. I was wrong about him. Sorry, James. I shouldn't have picked on him like I did."

"I bet he's smarter than most of us, actually," said Asher, who'd been listening. Asher held up Donner to admire how cute he was and then brought him back to his chest.

Mason grinned. "I bet you're right."

"I'm glad you think so, guys," said James. "Thanks, Mason. That means a lot."

Mason began to set up a display of giant candy canes in the yard that the dogs had knocked over, still gripping Blitzen in one arm.

James picked up a string of lights from the ground that had gone out and began to hook together a few other wires that had been pulled apart. Soon, his gaze fell on the red-and-white-striped candy cane display that Mason was arranging. "Guys, I have an idea."

All three boys stopped what they were

doing to exchange a questioning look.

James plugged the long string of lights into one last wire and suddenly, the whole string of beautiful white lights came back on. A smile crept across his face. "And I think it just might work."

From the darkness behind, Ian jogged up. "Hey, guys!" He still held Cupid in his jacket. The boys greeted their friend, and Cupid yipped with joy when he saw his four-legged brothers. "Good news—I talked to some people back there who said the owners of the neighborhood dogs are out here looking for them. They're just a few blocks back."

"With leashes, I hope?" Asher asked.

"Yeah!" said Ian.

"Perfect!" said James. "Then, all we need to do is get the dogs to stay in one place and wait for backup. And it sounds like backup should be here soon."

"But how are we going to do that?" asked Ian.

"And where?" asked Mason.

"Trust me." James started toward the sidewalk. "I know just the place. Come on, guys. And come on, Rosco! We're going to need you."

CHAPTER 21

THE LEADER
OF THE PACK

Out on the sidewalk, James bent down to address Rosco. "Hey boy, remember when Mason and I found you this week on your own? We blamed you for knocking over a plastic snowman."

Rosco listened eagerly, panting. He remembered well. He did knock over that snowman.

James continued. "If you could make the pack of dogs follow you, could you lead them there?"

The boys listened closely, each holding a puppy. Even the puppies grew still. They seemed to sense something important was happening.

Rosco barked. He understood. He could do it. Off he ran.

James clapped his hands. "Come on, guys. Let's meet him there. It's not far but we have to hurry. Mason, is your leg okay? Can I have my bike back now?"

"Sure. Yeah, it feels a little better," said Mason, lifting the bike from the ground. "Take it!"

* * *

Rosco raced down the sidewalk in the direction the pack had last been seen. Before long, he came upon them. After a long evening on the run, the dogs had begun to tire. The Bulldog had fallen to the back and the Rottweiler had taken over the lead. The tiny Pomeranian was struggling to keep up. Even Sparks, as determined as he was, had finally slowed to nothing more than a fast walk. Rosco cut in next to him.

Sparks yipped, surprised and relieved to see his friend. *Rosco! What's up, pal?*

Rosco quickly <u>relayed</u> the plan and Sparks <u>retreated</u> to the back, happy that help had finally arrived. Rosco raced to the front.

Surprised to have a brand new leader, the dogs responded with fresh enthusiasm and picked up their pace. Rosco turned and headed in the other direction. The pack followed closely.

* * *

Rounding a bend, the boys glimpsed the yard that was their destination. James zipped ahead. Reaching it first, he dropped his bike and ran to the gate.

As usual, the gate was open, beckoning visitors inside its bright and sparkling, red-and-white-lined yard.

Mason and the others hurried to catch up as the pack appeared from the other direction.

"Here they come!" shouted Ian.

Wasting no time, Rosco circled down the sidewalk and through the gate. The eager pack of dogs raced in behind him.

"He's doing it—he's taking them in there!" said Mason. "It's working!"

"Yee-haw!" Asher yelled. "Go, Rosco!"

"Get ready, James!" Ian called.

"I'm on it!" James grabbed the gate. When the last of the neighborhood pack ran inside, followed by Sparks, James shut the gate and locked it.

Once penned in the yard, the dogs slowed down. They sniffed at the snowman and the yard's other decorations with interest.

"Wow—he did it!" cried Asher as the boys arrived on the scene. "Rosco did it!"

It seemed that being placed in a confined space had brought the dogs back to their senses. It had reminded them that they weren't wild dogs after all, that they were pets with good manners who had front yards of their own, not so different from this one.

Sparks huffed and puffed, thirsty and out of breath. He watched with satisfaction as Rosco sniffed noses <u>cordially</u> with the Bulldog and the Boxer. Sparks sat down on the grass near the Pomeranian. Together they panted, glad for a rest. *At last, it's over,* thought Sparks, and he fell onto his side, exhausted.

Soon, the owner of the house came out with bowls full of cold water for the thirsty dogs. The dogs waited their turns then lapped at the water.

A few minutes later, Mrs. Taylor pulled up to the curb and parked. Sarah burst from the passenger side. She ran up to Ian and scooped Cupid from him without asking. "Thank you so much!" she said. "I have been so worried about them!"

"Uh, you're welcome?" said Ian. "I take it these are yours?"

"Oh, sorry. Yes, these are our puppies!" She hugged Cupid like he'd been gone for years.

Mrs. Taylor hurried around from the other side of the car. She was still limping in only one heel, and reached out to Leo with both hands, an expectant look across her face. "May I?"

Leo shrugged, not quite sure what to say. "I guess so." Reluctantly, he handed Comet over to her.

"Oh, thank you so much, boys, for taking good care of our little angels! We went after them on foot for as long as we could, but had to adjust our strategy because of my silly boots!" She held up her foot to show them.

The boys laughed.

"We were already starting to get desperate when this silly thing broke. That's when we finally decided to walk back and get the car. But then driving through this slow line of traffic took *forever*! Oh—I'm so glad we finally found you! We've both been so worried!"

After retrieving leashes from the back seat of the car, Mrs. Taylor hooked them to the puppies' collars. The puppies tried to scatter, but this time they couldn't get far from the sidewalk. She squatted down to pet them. "Comet, Cupid, Donner, and Blitzen, I hope you didn't cause too much trouble tonight. What am I ever going to do with you four?" She turned to Sarah. "I guess we'll have to wait until next year to take pictures with their leashes off, won't we, honey?"

"Oh, so that's how this all happened?" James nodded slowly. "That makes sense..."

Sarah pulled out her phone and snapped a few photos. "Oh well, I don't mind leashes in the picture anymore." She grinned. "It's better than letting them run off again."

"You can say *that* again," said Asher.

"Wait, those are their names?" asked Ian. Like, Santa's reindeer?"

"Yes!" Sarah answered. "We named them that way because they were early Christmas presents from my dad. Isn't that so cute?"

"It's adorable," said Mason.

Asher laughed. "Well, that explains why they liked playing on the Christmas decorations so much!"

"Again, boys, we can't thank you enough for rescuing them! And we're so sorry for any messes they might have made out here," Mrs. Taylor said. "Now, let's get these tired, little babies home to bed."

The boys waved with sad faces as the Taylors drove away. They'd already grown attached to the sweet little puppies and were going to miss them.

Before long, the neighborhood dog owners arrived and expressed their gratitude to the boys. "I wasn't sure how we'd ever catch them," said one of the men. "They took off like lightning. Thank you, boys! We're so sorry they almost ruined our opening night!"

"But, luckily, they didn't," said Mr. Da Costa, who had joined them in pursuit of the dogs. "By the way, James, I looked in on the party at your house and told your dad what was happening out here. It seems that he has been keeping the contest judges <u>distracted</u> all evening. They don't know a thing about tonight's events."

"Whew!" said James. "That's a relief. Thanks, Mr. Da Costa!"

"Sure. Oh, and James, your dad said to give you a message. He said to tell you—"

Just then Mr. McKendrick hurried down the sidewalk toward them, speaking into his walkie-talkie, with a sly grin across his face since he didn't actually need to use it. "I said to tell you that I'm very proud of you, and that I can't wait to hear all about it tonight."

"Dad, you're here!" James threw his arms around his dad's waist.

"Yes, I finally made it!"

Mandy ran up from behind her father. "James, we sold out of hot chocolate, completely!" She had eventually closed down the stand and joined her dad to search for James and the boys. "I ran the stand all by myself for a while, and then Mrs. Benton came to help! It was fun!"

"Really? Wow! Great job, Mandy!" James high-fived his sister. "I knew you could do it."

"Dad, you won't believe how bad it got out there," said James. "I'm sorry I didn't radio you when it all started. I just thought I could handle it by myself."

"Don't worry about it, son," said Mr. McKendrick. "When I heard what was going on earlier, I went outside to go and find you. But the neighbors stopped me—they said you boys were taking care of things, and that I'd better not leave because it might make the judges suspicious, so I decided to wait it out. I was really nervous about it, but I should've known you guys would've solved the problem on your own."

He ruffled James' red hair. "I knew I could count on you." He patted Mason on the back. "You too, Mason. You two make a great team."

"Us five, you mean," said James.

"Yes, you five, it would seem!" Mr. McKendrick thanked the other boys.

"Thanks, Mr. M," said Mason and the others.

Ian exchanged a fist bump with Asher and Leo, and Mr. McKendrick joined the other adults in conversation.

"I think Rosco deserves some thanks, too," said Asher. We might still be chasing the big dogs if he hadn't been able to lead them inside this fence. Come here, Rosco! Come and let me pat you on the back!"

Rosco trotted over, tongue dripping with water. Asher reached over the fence to pet him.

"Well, in all fairness Rosco did kinda start this trouble," said James. "But I'm pretty sure he didn't mean to."

Mason grinned. "That's true, and after all, he *did* stop it." He reached down to pet Rosco over the fence. Rosco panted, a wide grin across his face. "I'm sorry again that I made fun of Rosco, James. I should've known he wasn't trying to cause trouble. He's a really great dog."

Mandy gave James a wide smile at Mason's comment, then she and the other boys went inside the yard to play with the neighborhood dogs. James turned to Mason. "Look, dude. You do come up with some really good ideas. I shouldn't get all mad when you take charge of things."

"It's okay, James. I'm sorry I took over. I don't always realize I'm doing that. I should've asked you first before I invited the guys."

"It's okay." James picked up a stick from the grass and threw it across the yard for Rosco to fetch. "You were right, Mason—it *was* more fun with everybody here." He shrugged his shoulders. "Besides, if you hadn't taken things over tonight, I might still be chasing a pack of wild dogs around the block by myself."

Mason smiled. "Not to mention trying to catch more puppies than one person can carry."

"And look," said James, "I'm sorry, too. I shouldn't have tried to take so much credit. I was acting like I won the contest by myself. But I didn't."

"You helped, though." Mason put together a finger and thumb to demonstrate a tiny amount. "You and your dad—little bit."

James laughed.

"I'm kidding, of course. We wouldn't have even *been* in the contest without you and your dad," said Mason. "Everyone knows that."

Mandy skipped over, having heard the end of the conversation. "That's the understatement of the year, Mason."

"Wow, that's a big word for such a little girl."

"I'm not *little*!" Mandy put her hands on her hips and stuck out her tongue at him. Mason laughed, then Mandy giggled.

James took the stick from Rosco, surprised that he had brought it back so swiftly. He threw it again, but this time, Rosco ran off with it and didn't return. *Now that's the dog I'm used to.* James smiled. Taking first place had caused him to lose sight of what really mattered. He'd gotten so caught up in it all.

The contest wasn't about who had the

brightest lights or the best decorations. It wasn't about winning at all. It was about spreading joy—lots of it, to anyone who cared to wander through the neighborhood, all season long.

* * *

On the other side of the yard, a lively game of chase was taking place. A tall brown Labradoodle chased a small but quick Australian terrier, who chased Sparks. Rosco smiled, panting. He wanted to get in on the fun. Within seconds he joined the group on the heels of the Labradoodle.

Rosco sped around the yard. He was satisfied with himself. He had proven himself a trouble-stopper in the eyes of Mason and the rest of the kids. He had restored James' faith in him.

"Ruff, ruff!" Sparks yipped. *Merry Christmas, Rosco!*

Rosco barked back. *Merry Christmas, Sparks!*

Best of all, Rosco finally understood why

the people had decorated the neighborhood to look so beautiful and feel so cheerful. He finally understood why it mattered so much to James and Mason and everybody else. He finally understood why they'd want to hold the title of Best Block even just once.

The lights, the amazing displays in the neighborhood—indeed, the whole contest— was just one of the ways that people and dogs could share the joy of the Christmas season with each other. That was, surely, the *best*.

Quick-Look Vocabulary

Although some words in the English language have more than one definition, the definitions below explain *only* the way the word is used within *this* story. The following words are underlined in the book to make it easy to look them up here.

address - verb: to speak to

astonished - adj.: surprised

aw, fiddlesticks - an expression meaning *oh, drat* or *doggone it*

barrel - verb: to move fast, not concerned with surrounding conditions

bound - verb: to leap, jump, or spring

brimming - adj.: to be full of

buckle - verb: to bend or collapse

chaotic - adj.: extremely confused or disorderly

chaos - noun: extreme confusion

commotion - noun: a noisy disturbance

contentedly - adv.: feeling satisfied

cordially - adv.: gracious, friendly, warm

cringe - verb: to shrink back because one dislikes or is disgusted by something

decorative - adj.: fancy, pretty, serving to decorate something

distract - verb: to draw attention away from something

distraction - noun: something that prevents concentration, an interruption

emerge - verb: to come out, arise

fare - verb: to experience good or bad fortune; to do

festive - adj.: cheerful, merry, joyful

gape - verb: to stare with open mouth, as in wonder

glum - adj.: gloomy, sad

guilty as charged - an expression meaning the offender is guilty of what he has been accused of doing

idiotic - adj.: acting dumb or stupid like an idiot

impart - verb: to give or share information

incident - noun: something that happens or occurs; an event

inflatable - adj.: being hollow and enlarged with air or gas

laughingstock - noun: someone or something being laughed at

mishmash - noun: a confused mess, a hodgepodge, a jumble

ornamental - adj.: used for decoration

oversized - adj.: really big

pitiful - adj.: deserving sorrow or regret; low, despicable

rampage - noun: violent, excited, or reckless behavior

relay - verb: to explain or tell; to provide information

retreat - verb: to withdraw or fall back

shipshape - adj.: arranged well; tidy.

sightseers - noun: those who go about seeing the major sights of a place

spoke - noun: one of the bars, rods, or rungs radiating from the hub of a wheel on a bicycle

stake - noun: a post in the ground to which a rope or line can be tied

state-of-the-art - adj.: the latest and most advanced stage of a technology

steal the show - an expression that means to take the attention away from another

study – noun: a room in a house or other building, set apart for reading, writing, or working

tongue-tied - adj.: unable to speak, as from shyness, embarrassment, or surprise

topple - verb: to become unsteady and fall

understatement - noun: a statement that presents something as less important than it really is

upright - adj.: positioned vertically; standing up

wince - verb: a slight physical reaction; to draw back in alarm or disgust

Spelling Bee

Quiz your friends or practice these words and impress your teacher this holiday season!

yuletide

fruitcake

gift exchange

reindeer

decoration

charity

cheerfulness

poinsettia

Noel

icicles

tinsel

chimney

cranberry

sleigh

anticipation

wrapping paper

Dog Breeds

Several different dog breeds were mentioned in the book. Would you be able to spot each of these dogs if you saw one?

German shepherd

Pug

Boxer

Rottweiler

Pomeranian

Labradoodle

Bulldog

Australian terrier

Border collie

About the Author

Shana Gorian, originally from western Pennsylvania, lives in Southern California with her husband, two children, and her German shepherd, Rugger, the real *Rosco*. Like the McKendricks, Shana and her family tour their local holiday lights contest every year, enjoying Christmas songs in the car while sipping mugs of steaming hot chocolate.

Ros Webb is an artist based in Ireland. She has produced a multitude of work for books, digital books and websites. Samples of her art can be seen at https://www.facebook.com/TheChildrensBookIllustrator/

Josh Addessi is a quirky illustrator and animation professor based in Northwest Indiana. He has digitally painted all manner of book covers, stage backdrops, and trading cards. Samples of his art can be seen at http://joshaddessi.blogspot.com/

The *real* Rosco the Rascal, Rugger (pronounced Rooger), is every bit as loveable and rascally as Rosco. He loves to run in packs, look at Christmas lights, and chase squirrels, too.

Visit **shanagorian.com** to keep up with Rosco and his upcoming adventures, and don't miss the other books in the series!

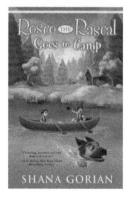

CPSIA information can be obtained
at www.ICGtesting.com
Printed in the USA
LVHW091726260319
611890LV00003B/588/P